A Rare Benedictine

A Rare Benedictine

Ellis Peters

THE MYSTERIOUS PRESS

New York • London • Tokyo • Sweden

First published in Great Britain in 1988 by Headline Book Publishing PLC

 The Mysterious Press, 129 West 56th Street, New York, N.Y. 10019

Printed in the United States of America
First U.S.A. Printing: November 1989
10 9 8 7 6 5 4 3 2 1

Library of Congress Cataloging-in-Publication Data

Peters, Ellis, 1913–
   A rare benedictine / Ellis Peters.
      p.   cm
   ISBN 0-89296-397-2
   I. Title.
PR6031.A49R37   1989
823'.912--dc20   89-42603
                                                                          CIP

Designed by Giorgetta Bell McRee

Contents

Introduction   1

A Light on the Road to Woodstock   5

The Price of Light   43

Eye Witness   77

A Rare Benedictine

Introduction

Brother Cadfael sprang to life suddenly and unexpectedly when he was already approaching sixty, mature, experienced, fully armed and seventeen years tonsured. He emerged as the necessary protagonist when I had the idea of deriving a plot for a murder mystery from the true history of Shrewsbury Abbey in the twelfth century, and needed the high mediaeval equivalent of a detective, an observer and agent of justice in the centre of the action. I had no idea then what I was launching on the world, nor to how demanding a mentor I was subjecting myself. Nor did I intend a series of books about him, indeed I went on immediately to write a modern detective novel, and returned to the twelfth century and Shrewsbury only when I could no longer resist the temptation to shape another book round the siege of Shrewsbury and the massacre of the garrison by King Stephen, which followed shortly after the prior's expedition into Wales to bring back the relics of Saint Winifred for his Abbey. From then on Brother Cadfael was well into his stride, and there was no turning back.

Since the action in the first book was almost all in Wales, and even in succeeding ones went back and forth freely across the border, just as the history of Shrewsbury always has, Cadfael had to be Welsh, and very much at home there. His name was chosen as being so rare that I can find it only once in Welsh history, and even in that instance it disappears almost as soon as it is bestowed in baptism. Saint Cadog, contemporary and rival of Saint David, a powerful saint in Glamorgan, was actually christened Cadfael, but ever after seems to have been "familiarly known," as Sir John Lloyd says, as Cadog. A name of which the saint had no further need, and which appears, as far as I know, nowhere else, seemed just the thing for my man. No implication of saintliness was intended, though indeed when affronted Saint Cadog seems to have behaved with the unforgiving ferocity of most of his kind, at least in legend. My monk had to be a man of wide worldly experience and an inexhaustible fund of resigned tolerance for the human condition. His crusading and seafaring past, with all its enthusiasms and disillusionments, was referred to from the beginning. Only later did readers begin to wonder and ask about his former roving life, and how and why he became a monk.

For reasons of continuity I did not wish to go back in time and write a book about his crusading days. Whatever else may be true of it, the entire sequence of novels proceeds steadily season by season, year by year, in a progressive tension which I did not want to break. But when I had the opportunity to cast a glance behind by way of a short story, to shed light on his vocation, I was glad to use it.

So here he is, not a convert, for this is not a conversion. In an age of relatively uncomplicated faith, not yet obsessed and tormented by cantankerous schisms, sects and politicians, Cadfael has always been an unquestioning believer. What happens to him on the road to Woodstock is simply the acceptance of a revelation from within that the life he has lived to date, active, mobile and often violent, has reached its natural end, and he is confronted by a new need and a different challenge.

In India it is not unknown for a man who has possessed great power and wealth to discard everything when he reaches a certain age—recognisable to him when it comes not by dates and times, but by an inward certainty—put on the yellow robe of a sannyasi, and go away with nothing but a begging bowl, at once into the world and out of it.

Given the difference in climate and tradition between the saffron robe and the voluminous black habit, the solitary with the wilderness for his cloister, and the wall suddenly enclosing and embracing the traveller over half the world, that is pretty much what Cadfael does in entering the Rule of Saint Benedict in the Abbey of Saint Peter and Saint Paul, at Shrewsbury.

Thereafter, on occasions and for what he feels to be good reasons, he may break the rules. He will never transgress against the Rule, and never abandon it.

Ellis Peters, 1988

A Light on the Road to Woodstock

he King's court was in no hurry to return to England, that late autumn of 1120, even though the fighting, somewhat desultory in these last stages, was long over, and the enforced peace sealed by a royal marriage. King Henry had brought to a successful conclusion his sixteen years of patient cunning, relentless plotting, fighting and manipulating, and could now sit back in high content, master not only of England but of Normandy, too. What the Conqueror had misguidedly dealt out in two separate parcels to his two elder sons, his youngest son had now put together again and clamped into one. Not without a hand in removing from the light of day, some said, both of his brothers, one of whom had been shovelled into a hasty grave under the tower at Winchester, while the other

was now a prisoner in Devizes, and unlikely ever to be seen again by the outer world.

The court could well afford to linger to enjoy victory, while Henry trimmed into neatness the last loose edges still to be made secure. But his fleet was already preparing at Barfleur for the voyage back to England, and he would be home before the month ended. Meantime, many of his barons and knights who had fought his battles were withdrawing their contingents and making for home, among them one Roger Mauduit, who had a young and handsome wife waiting for him, certain legal business on his mind, and twenty-five men to ship back to England, most of them to be paid off on landing.

There were one or two among the miscellaneous riff-raff he had recruited here in Normandy on his lord's behalf whom it might be worth keeping on in his own service, along with the few men of his household, at least until he was safely home. The vagabond clerk turned soldier, let him be unfrocked priest or what he might, was an excellent copyist and a sound Latin scholar, and could put legal documents in their best and most presentable form, in good time for the King's court at Woodstock. And the Welsh man-at-arms, blunt and insubordinate as he was, was also experienced and accomplished in arms, a man of his word, once given, and utterly reliable in whatever situation on land or sea, for in both elements he had long practice behind him. Roger was well aware that he was not greatly loved, and had little faith in either the valour or the loyalty of his own men. But this Welshman from Gwynedd, by way of Antioch and Jerusalem and only God knew where else, had imbibed the code of arms and wore it as a second nature. With or without love, such service as he pledged, that he would provide.

Roger put it to them both as his men were embarking at Barfleur, in the middle of a deceptively placid November, and upon a calm sea.

"I would have you two accompany me to my manor of Sutton Mauduit by Northampton, when we disembark, and stay in my pay until a certain lawsuit I have against the abbey of Shrewsbury is resolved. The King intends to come to Woodstock when he arrives in England, and will be there to preside over my case on the twenty-third day of this month. Will you remain in my service until that day?"

The Welshman said that he would, until that day or until the case was resolved. He said it indifferently, as one who has no business of any importance anywhere in the world to pull him in another direction. As well Northampton as anywhere else. As well Woodstock. And after Woodstock? Why anywhere in particular? There was no identifiable light beckoning him anywhere, along any road. The world was wide, fair and full of savour, but without signposts.

Alard, the tatterdemalion clerk, hesitated, scratched his thick thatch of grizzled red hair, and finally also said yes, but as if some vague regret drew him in another direction. It meant pay for some days more; he could not afford to say no.

"I would have gone with him with better heart," he said later, when they were leaning on the rail together, watching the low blue line of the English shore rise out of a placid sea, "if he had been taking a more westerly road."

"Why that?" asked Cadfael ap Meilyr ap Dafydd. "Have you kin in the west?"

"I had once. I have not now."

"Dead?"

"I am the one who died." Alard heaved lean shoulders in a helpless shrug, and grinned. "Fifty-seven brothers I had, and now I'm brotherless. I begin to miss my kin, now I'm past forty. I never valued them when I was young." He slanted a rueful glance at his companion and shook his head. "I was a monk of Evesham, an *oblatus*, given to God by my father when I was five years old. When I was fifteen I could no longer abide to live my life in one place, and I ran. Stability is one of the vows we take—to be content in one stay, and go abroad only when ordered. That was not for me, not then. My sort they call *vagus*—frivolous minds that must wander. Well, I've wandered far enough, God knows, in my time. I begin to fear I can never stand still again."

The Welshman drew his cloak about him against the chill of the wind. "Are you hankering for a return?"

"Even you seamen must drop anchor somewhere at last," said Alard. "They'd have my hide if I went back, that I know. But there's this about penance, it pays all debts, and leaves the record clear. They'd find a place for me, once I'd paid. But I don't know . . . I don't know. . . . The *vagus* is still in me. I'm torn two ways."

"After twenty-five years," said Cadfael, "a month or two more for quiet thinking can do no harm. Copy his papers for him and take your case until his business is settled."

They were much of an age, though the renegade monk looked the elder by ten years, and much knocked about by the world he had coveted from within the cloister. It had never paid him well in goods or gear, for he went threadbare and thin, but in wisdom he might have got his fair wages. A little soldiering, a little clerking, some horse-tending, any labour that came to hand, until he could turn his hand to almost anything a hale man can do. He had seen, he said, Italy as far south as Rome, served once for a time under the Count of Flanders, crossed the mountains into Spain, never abiding anywhere for long. His feet still served him, but his mind grew weary of the road.

"And you?" he said, eyeing his companion, whom he had known now for a year in this last campaign. "You're something of a *vagus* yourself, by your own account. All those years crusading and battling corsairs in the midland sea, and still you have not enough of it, but must cross the sea again to get buffeted about Normandy. Had you no better business of your own, once you got back to England, but you must enlist again in this muddled mêlée of a war? No woman to take your mind off fighting?"

"What of yourself? Free of the cloister, free of the vows!"

"Somehow," said Alard, himself puzzled, "I never saw it so. A woman here and there, yes, when the heat was on me, and there was a woman by and willing, but marriage and wiving . . . it never seemed to me I had the right."

The Welshman braced his feet on the gently swaying deck and watched the distant shore draw nearer. A broad-set, sturdy, muscular man in his healthy prime, brown-haired and brown-skinned from eastern suns and outdoor living, well-provided in leather coat and good cloth, and well-armed with sword and dagger. A comely enough face, strongly featured, with the bold bones of his race—there had been women, in his time, who had found him handsome.

"I had a girl," he said meditatively, "years back, before ever I went crusading. But I left her when I took the Cross, left her for three years and stayed away seventeen. The truth is, in the east I forgot her, and in the west she, thanks be to God, had forgotten me. I did enquire, when I got back. She'd made a better bargain, and married a decent, solid man who had nothing of the *vagus* in him. A guildsman and counsellor of the town of Shrewsbury, no less. So I shed the load from my conscience and went back to what I knew, soldiering. With no regrets," he said simply. "It was all over and done, years since. I doubt if I should have known her again, or she me." There had been other women's faces in the years between, still vivid in his memory, while hers had faded into mist.

"And what will you do," asked Alard, "now the King's got everything he wanted, married his son to Anjou and Maine, and made an end of fighting? Go back to the east? There's never any want of squabbles there to keep a man busy."

"No," said Cadfael, eyes fixed on the shore that began to show the solidity of land and the undulations of cliff and down. For that, too, was over and done, years since, and not as well done as once he had hoped. This desultory campaigning in Normandy was little more than a postscriptum, an afterthought, a means of filling in the interim between what was past and what was to come, and as yet unrevealed. All he knew of it was that it must be something new and momentous, a door opening into another room. "It seems we have both a few days' grace, you and I, to find out where we are going. We'd best make good use of the time."

There was stir enough before night to keep them from wondering beyond the next moment, or troubling their minds about what was past or what was to come. Their ship put into the roads with a steady and favourable wind, and made course into Southampton before the light faded, and there was work for Alard checking the gear as it was unloaded, and for Cadfael disembarking the horses. A night's sleep in lodgings and stables in the town, and they would be on their way with the dawn.

"So the King's due in Woodstock," said Alard, rustling sleepily in his straw in a warm loft over the horses, "in time to sit in judgement on the twenty-third of the month. He makes his forest lodges the hub of his kingdom, there's more statecraft talked at Woodstock, so they say, than ever at Westminster. And he keeps his beasts there—lions and leopards—even camels. Did you ever see camels, Cadfael? There in the east?"

"Saw them and rode them. Common as horses there, hard-working and serviceable, but uncomfortable riding, and foul-tempered. Thank God it's horses we'll be mounting in the morning." And after a long silence, on the edge of sleep, he asked curiously into the straw-scented darkness: "If ever you do go back, what is it you want of Evesham?"

"Do I know?" responded Alard drowsily, and followed that with a sudden sharpening sigh, again fully awake. "The silence, it might be . . . or the stillness. To have no more running to do . . . to have arrived, and have no more need to run. The appetite changes. Now I think it would be a beautiful thing to be still."

The manor which was the head of Roger Mauduit's scattered and substantial honour lay somewhat south-east of North-ampton, comfortably under the lee of the long ridge of wooded hills where the king had a chase, and spreading its extensive fields over the rich lowland between. The house was of stone, and ample, over a deep undercroft, and with a low tower providing two small chambers at the eastern end, and the array of sturdy byres, barns, and stables that lined the containing walls was impressive. Someone had proved a good steward while the lord was away about King Henry's business.

The furnishings of the hall were no less eloquent of good management, and the men and maids of the household went about their work with a brisk wariness that showed they went in some awe of whoever presided over their labours. It needed only a single day of watching the Lady Eadwina in action to show who ruled the roost here. Roger Mauduit had married a wife not only handsome, but also efficient and masterful. She had had her own way here for three years, and by all the signs had enjoyed her dominance. She might, even, be none too glad to resign her charge now, however glad she might be to have her lord home again.

She was a tall, graceful woman, ten years younger than Roger, with an abundance of fair hair, and large blue eyes that went discreetly half-veiled by absurdly long lashes most of the time, but flashed a bright and steely challenge when she opened them fully. Her smile was likewise discreet and almost constant, concealing rather than revealing whatever went on in her mind; and though her welcome to her returning lord left nothing to be desired, but lavished on him every possible tribute of ceremony and affection from the moment his horse entered at the gate, Cadfael could not but wonder whether she was not, at the same time, taking stock of every man he brought in with him, and every article of gear or harness or weaponry in their equipment, as one taking jealous inventory of his goods and reserves to make sure nothing was lacking.

She had her little son by the hand, a boy of about seven years old, and the child had the same fair colouring, the same contained and almost supercilious smile, and was as spruce and fine as his mother.

The lady received Alard with a sweeping glance that deprecated his tatterdemalion appearance and doubted his morality, but nevertheless was willing to accept and make use of his abilities. The clerk who kept the manor roll and the accounts was efficient enough, but had no Latin, and could not write a good court hand. Alard was whisked away to a small table set in the angle of the great hearth, and kept hard at work copying certain charters and letters, and preparing them for presentation.

"This suit of his is against the abbey of Shrewsbury," said Alard, freed of his labours after supper in hall. "I recall you said that girl of yours had married a merchant in that town. Shrewsbury is a Benedictine house, like mine of Evesham." His, he called it still, after so many years of abandoning it; or his again, after time had brushed away whatever division there had ever been. "You must know it, if you come from there."

"I was born in Trefriw, in Gwynedd," said Cadfael, "but I took service early with an English wool-merchant, and came to Shrewsbury with his household. Fourteen, I was then—in Wales fourteen is manhood, and as I was a good lad with the short bow, and took kindly to the sword, I suppose I was worth my keep. The best of my following years were spent in Shrewsbury, I know it like my own palm, abbey and all. My master sent me there a year and more, to get my letters. But I quit that service when he died. I'd pledged nothing to the son, and he was a poor shadow of his father. That was when I took the Cross. So did many like me, all afire. I won't say what followed was all ash, but it burned very low at times."

"It's Mauduit who holds this disputed land," said Alard, "and the abbey that sues to recover it, and the thing's been going on four years without a settlement, ever since the old man here died. From what I know of the Benedictines, I'd rate their honesty above our Roger's, I tell you straight. And yet his charters seem to be genuine, as far as I can tell."

"Where is this land they're fighting over?" asked Cadfael.

"It's a manor by the name of Rotesley, near Stretton, demesne, village, advowson of the church and all. It seems when the great earl was just dead and his abbey still building, Roger's father gave Rotesley to the abbey. No dispute about that, the charter's there to show it. But the abbey granted it back to him as tenant for life, to live out his latter years there undisturbed, Roger being then married and installed here at Sutton. That's where the dispute starts. The abbey claims it was clearly agreed the tenancy ended with the old man's death, that he himself understood it so, and intended it should be restored to the abbey as soon as he was out of it. While Roger says there was no such agreement to restore it unconditionally, but the tenancy was granted to the Mauduits, and ought to be hereditary. And so far he's hung on to it tooth and claw. After several hearings they remitted it to the King himself. And that's why you and I, my friend, will be off with his lordship to Woodstock the day after tomorrow."

"And how do you rate his chances of success? He seems none too sure himself," said Cadfael, "to judge by his short temper and nailbiting this last day or so."

"Why, the charter could have been worded better. It says simply that the village is granted back in tenancy during the old man's lifetime, but fails to say anything about what shall happen afterwards, whatever may have been intended. From what I hear, they were on very good terms, Abbot Fulchered and the old lord, agreements between them on other matters in the manor book are worded as between men who trusted each other. The witnesses are all of them dead, as Abbot Fulchered is dead. It's one Godefrid now. But for all I know the abbey may hold letters that have passed between

the two, and a letter is witness of intent, no less than a
formal charter. All in good time we shall see."

The nobility still sat at the high table, in no haste to retire,
Roger brooding over his wine, of which he had already
drunk his fair share and more. Cadfael eyed them with
interest, seen thus in a family setting. The boy had gone to
his bed, hauled away by an elderly nurse, but the Lady
Eadwina sat in close attendance at her lord's left hand, and
kept his cup well filled, smiling her faint, demure smile. On
her left sat a very fine young squire of about twenty-five
years, deferential and discreet, with a smile somehow the
male reflection of her own. The source of both was secret; the
spring of their pleasure or amusement, or whatever caused
them so to smile, remained private and slightly unnerving,
like the carved stone smiles of certain very old statues
Cadfael had seen in Greece, long ago. For all his mild,
amiable and ornamental appearance, combed and curled and
courtly, he was a big, well-set-up young fellow, with a set to
his smooth jaw. Cadfael studied him with interest, for he
was plainly privileged here.

"Goscelin," said Alard by way of explanation, following
his friend's glance. "Her right-hand man while Roger was
away."

Her left-hand man now, by the look of it, thought Cadfael.
For her left hand and Goscelin's right were private under
the table, while she spoke winningly into her husband's ear;
and if those two hands were not paddling palms at this
moment Cadfael was very much deceived. Above and below
the drapings of the board were two different worlds. "I
wonder," he said thoughtfully, "what she's breathing into
Roger's ear now."

What the lady was breathing into her husband's ear was,

in fact: "You fret over nothing, my lord. What does it matter how strong his proofs, if he never reaches Woodstock in time to present them? You know the law: if one party fails to appear, judgement is given for the other. The assize judges may allow more than one default if they please, but do you think King Henry will? Whoever fails of keeping tryst with him will be felled on the spot. And you know the road by which Prior Heribert must come." Her voice was a silken purr in his ear. "And have you not a hunting-lodge in the forest north of Woodstock, through which that road passes?"

Roger's hand had stiffened round the stem of his wine cup. He was not so drunk but he was listening intently.

"Shrewsbury to Woodstock will be a two- or three-day journey to such a rider. All you need do is have a watcher on the road north of you, to give warning. The woods are thick enough, masterless men have been known to haunt there. Even if he comes by daylight, your part need never be known. Hide him but a few days, it will be long enough. Then turn him loose by night, and who's ever to know what footpads held and robbed him? You need not even touch his parchments—robbers would count them worthless. Take what common thieves would take, and theirs will be the blame."

Roger opened his tight-shut mouth to say in a doubtful growl: "He'll not be travelling alone."

"Hah! Two or three abbey servants—they'll run like hares. You need not trouble yourself over them. Three stout, silent men of your own will be more than enough."

He brooded, and began to think so, too, and to review in his mind the men of his household, seeking the right hands for such work. Not the Welshman and the clerk, the strangers here; their part was to be the honest onlookers, in case there should ever be questions asked.

They left Sutton Mauduit on the twentieth day of November, which seemed unnecessarily early, though as Roger had decreed that they should settle in his hunting-lodge in the forest close by Woodstock, which meant conveying stores with them to make the house habitable and provision it for a party for, presumably, a stay of three nights at least, it was perhaps a wise precaution. Roger was taking no chances in his suit, he said; he meant to be established on the ground in good time, and have all his proofs in order.

"But so he has," said Alard, pricked in his professional pride, "for I've gone over everything with him, and the case, if open in default of specific instructions, is plain enough and will stand up. What the abbey can muster, who knows? They say the abbot is not well, which is why his prior comes in his place. My work is done."

He had the faraway look in his eye, as the party rode out and faced westward, of one either penned and longing to be where he could but see, or loose and weary and being drawn home. Either a *vagus* escaping outward, or a penitent flying back in haste before the doors should close against him. There must indeed be something desirable and lovely to cause a man to look towards it with that look on his face.

Three men-at-arms and two grooms accompanied Roger, in addition to Alard and Cadfael, whose term of service would end with the session in court, after which they might go where they would, Cadfael horsed, since he owned his own mount, Alard afoot, since the pony he rode belonged to Roger. It came as something of a surprise to Cadfael that the squire Goscelin should also saddle up and ride with the party, very debonair and well-armed with sword and dagger.

"I marvel," said Cadfael drily, "that the lady doesn't need him at home for her own protection, while her lord's absent."

The Lady Eadwina, however, bade farewell to the whole party with the greatest serenity, and to her husband with demonstrative affection, putting forward her little son to be embraced and kissed. Perhaps, thought Cadfael, relenting, I do her wrong, simply because I feel chilled by that smile of hers. For all I know she may be the truest wife living.

They set out early, and before Buckingham, made a halt at the small and penurious priory of Bradwell, where Roger elected to spend the night, keeping his three men-at-arms with him, while Goscelin with the rest of the party rode on to the hunting-lodge to make all ready for their lord's reception the following day. It was growing dark by the time they arrived, and the bustle of kindling fire and torches, and unloading the bed-linen and stores from the sumpter ponies went on into the night. The lodge was small, stockaded, well-furnished with stabling and mews, and in thick woodland, a place comfortable enough once they had a roaring fire on the hearth and food on the table.

"The road the prior of Shrewsbury will be coming by," said Alard, warming himself by the fire after supper, "passes through Evesham. As like as not they'll stay the last night there." With every mile west Cadfael had seen him straining forward with mounting eagerness. "The road cannot be far away from us here, it passes through this forest."

"It must be nearly thirty miles to Evesham," said Cadfael. "A long day's riding for a clerical party. It will be night by the time they ride past into Woodstock. If you're set on going, stay at least to get your pay, for you'll need it before the thirty miles is done."

They went to their slumber in the warmth of the hall without a word more said. But he would go, Alard, whether he himself knew it yet or not. Cadfael knew it. His friend was a tired horse with the scent of the stable in his nostrils; nothing would stop him now until he reached it.

It was well into the middle of the day when Roger and his escort arrived, and they approached not directly, as the advance party had done, but from the woods to the north, as though they had been indulging in a little hunting or hawking by the way, except that they had neither hawk nor hound with them. A fine, clear, cool day for riding, there was no reason in the world why they should not go roundabout for the pure pleasure of it—and indeed, they seemed to come in high content!—but that Roger's mind had been so preoccupied and so anxious concerning his lawsuit that distractions seemed unlikely. Cadfael was given to thinking about unlikely developments, which from old campaigns he knew to prove significant in most cases. Goscelin, who was out at the gate to welcome them in, was apparently oblivious to the direction from which they came. That way lay Alard's highway to his rest. But what meaning ought it to have for Roger Mauduit?

The table was lavish that night, and lord and squire drank well and ate well, and gave no sign of any care, though they might, Cadfael thought, watching them from his lower place, seem a little tight and knife-edged. Well, the King's court could account for that. Shrewsbury's prior was drawing steadily nearer, with whatever weapons he had for the battle. But it seemed rather an exultant tension than an anxious one. Was Roger counting his chickens already?

The morning of the twenty-second of November dawned, and the noon passed, and with every moment Alard's restlessness and abstraction grew, until with evening it possessed him utterly, and he could no longer resist. He presented himself before Roger after supper, when his mood might be mellow from good food and wine.

"My lord, with the morrow my service to you is completed. You need me no longer, and with your goodwill I would set forth now for where I am going. I go afoot and need provision for the road. If you have been content with my work, pay me what is due, and let me go."

It seemed that Roger had been startled out of some equally absorbing preoccupation of his own, and was in haste to return to it, for he made no demur, but paid at once. To do him justice, he had never been a grudging paymaster. He drove as hard a bargain as he could at the outset, but once the agreement was made, he kept it.

"Go when you please," he said. "Fill your bag from the kitchen for the journey when you leave. You did good work, I give you that."

And he returned to whatever it was that so engrossed his thoughts, and Alard went to collect the proffered largesse and his own meagre possessions.

"I am going," he said, meeting Cadfael in the hall doorway. "I must go." There was no more doubt in voice or face. "They will take me back, though in the lowest place. From that there's no falling. The blessed Benedict wrote in the Rule that even to the third time of straying a man may be received again if he promise full amendment."

It was a dark night, without moon or stars but in fleeting moments when the wind ripped apart the cloud covering to let through a brief gleam of moonlight. The weather had grown gusty and wild in the last two days; the King's fleet must have had a rough crossing from Barfleur.

"You'd do better," urged Cadfael, "to wait for morning, and go by daylight. Here's a safe bed, and the King's peace, however well enforced, hardly covers every mile of the King's highroads."

But Alard would not wait. The yearning was on him too strongly, and a penniless vagabond who had ventured all the roads of Christendom by day or night was hardly likely to flinch from the last thirty miles of his wanderings.

"Then I'll go with you as far as the road, and see you on your way," said Cadfael.

There was a mile or so of track through thick forest between them and the highroad that bore away west-north-west on the upland journey to Evesham. The ribbon of open highway, hemmed on both sides by trees, was hardly less dark than the forest itself. King Henry had fenced in his private park at Woodstock to house his wild beasts, but maintained also his hunting chase here, many miles in extent. At the road they parted, and Cadfael stood to watch his friend march steadily away towards the west, eyes fixed ahead, upon his penance and his absolution, a tired man with a rest assured.

Cadfael turned back towards the lodge as soon as the receding shadow had melted into the night. He was in no haste to go in, for the night, though blustery, was not cold, and he was in no mind to seek the company of others of the party now that the one best known to him was gone, and gone in so mysteriously rapt a fashion. He walked on among the trees, turning his back on his bed for a while.

The constant thrashing of branches in the wind all but drowned the scuffling and shouting that suddenly broke out behind him, at some distance among the trees, until a horse's shrill whinny brought him about with a jerk, and set him running through the underbrush towards the spot where confused voices yelled alarm and broken bushes thrashed. The clamour seemed some little way off, and he was startled as he shouldered his way headlong through a thicket to collide heavily with two entangled bodies, send them spinning apart, and himself fall a-sprawl upon one of them in the flattened grass. The man under him uttered a scared and angry cry, and the voice was Roger's. The other man had made no sound at all, but slid away very rapidly and lightly to vanish among the trees, a tall shadow swallowed in shadows.

Cadfael drew off in haste, reaching an arm to hoist the winded man. "My lord, are you hurt? What, in God's name, is to do here?" The sleeve he clutched slid warm and wet under his hand. "You're injured! Hold fast, let's see what harm's done before you move. . . ."

Then there was the voice of Goscelin, for once loud and vehement in alarm, shouting for his lord and crashing headlong through bush and brake to fall on his knees beside Roger, lamenting and raging.

"My lord, my lord, what happened here? What rogues were those, loose in the woods? Dared they waylay travellers so close to the King's highway? You're hurt—here's blood. . . ."

Roger got his breath back and sat up, feeling at his left arm below the shoulder, and wincing. "A scratch. My arm . . . God curse him, whoever he may be, the fellow struck for my heart. Man, if you had not come charging like a bull, I might have been dead. You hurled me off the point of his dagger. Thank God, there's no great harm, but I bleed. . . . Help me back home!"

"That a man may not walk by night in his own woods,"

fumed Goscelin, hoisting his lord carefully to his feet, "without being set upon by outlaws! Help here, you, Cadfael, take his other arm. . . . Footpads so close to Woodstock! Tomorrow we must turn out the watch to comb these tracks and hunt them out of cover, before they kill. . . ."

"Get me withindoors," snapped Roger, "and have this coat and shirt off me, and let's staunch this bleeding. I'm alive, that's the main!"

They helped him back between them, through the more open ways towards the lodge. It dawned on Cadfael, as they went, that the clamour of furtive battle had ceased completely, even the wind had abated, and somewhere on the road, distantly, he caught the rhythm of galloping hooves, very fast and light, as of a riderless horse in panic flight.

The gash in Roger Mauduit's left arm, just below the shoulder, was long but not deep, and grew shallower as it descended. The stroke that marked him thus could well have been meant for his heart. Cadfael's hurtling impact, at the very moment the attack was launched, had been the means of averting murder. The shadow that had melted into the night had no form, nothing about it rendered it human or recognisable. He had heard an outcry and run towards it, a projectile to strike attacked and attacker apart; questioned, that was all he could say.

For which, said Roger, bandaged and resting and warmed with mulled wine, he was heartily thankful. And indeed, Roger was behaving with remarkable fortitude and calm for a man who had just escaped death. By the time he had demonstrated to his dismayed grooms and men-at-arms that he was alive and not much the worse, appointed the hour when they should set out for Woodstock in the morning, and been helped to his bed by Goscelin, there was even a suggestion of complacency about him, as though a gash in the arm was a small price to pay for the successful retention of a valuable property and the defeat of his clerical opponents.

In the court of the palace of Woodstock the King's chamberlains, clerks and judges were fluttering about in a curiously distracted manner, or so it seemed to Cadfael, standing apart among the commoners to observe their antics. They gathered in small groups, conversing in low voices and with anxious faces, broke apart to regroup with others of their kind, hurried in and out among the litigants, avoiding or brushing off all questions, exchanged documents, hurried to the door to peer out, as if looking for some late arrival. And there was indeed one litigant who had not kept to his time, for there was no sign of a Benedictine prior among those assembled, nor had anyone appeared to explain or justify his absence. And Roger Mauduit, in spite of his stiff and painful arm, continued to relax, with ever-increasing assurance, into shining complacency.

The appointed hour was already some minutes past when four agitated fellows, two of them Benedictine brothers, made a hasty entrance, and accosted the presiding clerk.

"Sir," bleated the leader, loud in nervous dismay, "we here are come from the abbey of Shrewsbury, escort to our prior, who was on his way to plead a case at law here. Sir, you must hold him excused, for it is not his blame nor ours that he cannot appear. In the forest some two miles north, as we rode hither last night in the dark, we were attacked by a band of lawless robbers, and they have seized our prior and dragged him away. . . ."

The spokesman's voice had risen shrilly in his agitation; he had the attention of every man in the hall by this time. Certainly he had Cadfael's. Masterless men some two miles out of Woodstock, plying their trade last night, could only be the same who had happened upon Roger Mauduit and all but been the death of him. Any such gang, so close to the court, was astonishing enough, there could hardly be two. The clerk was outraged at the very idea.

"Seized and captured him? And you four were with him? Can this be true? How many were they who attacked you?"

"We could not tell for certain. Three at least—but they were lying in ambush, we had no chance to stand them off. They pulled him from his horse and were off into the trees with him. They knew the woods, and we did not. Sir, we did go after them, but they beat us off."

It was evident they had done their best, for two of them showed bruised and scratched, and all were soiled and torn as to their clothing.

"We have hunted through the night, but found no trace, only we caught his horse a mile down the highway as we came hither. So we plead here that our prior's absence be not seen as a default, for indeed he would have been here in the town last night if all had gone as it should."

"Hush, wait!" said the clerk peremptorily.

All heads had turned towards the door of the hall, where a great flurry of officials had suddenly surged into view, cleaving through the press with fixed and ominous haste, to take the centre of the floor below the King's empty dais. A chamberlain, elderly and authoritative, struck the floor loudly with his staff and commanded silence. And at sight of his face silence fell like a stone.

"My lords, gentlemen, all who have pleas here this day, and all others present, you are bidden to disperse, for there will be no hearings today. All suits that should be heard here must be postponed three days, and will be heard by His Grace's judges. His Grace the King cannot appear."

This time the silence fell again like a heavy curtain, muffling even thought or conjecture.

"The court is in mourning from this hour. We have received news of desolating import. His Grace with the greater part of his fleet made the crossing to England safely, as is known, but the *Blanche Nef*, in which His Grace's son and heir, Prince William, with all his companions and many other noble souls were embarked, put to sea late, and was caught in gales before ever clearing Barfleur. The ship is lost, split upon a rock, foundered with all hands, not a soul is come safe to land. Go hence quietly, and pray for the souls of the flower of this realm."

So that was the end of one man's year of triumph, an empty achievement, a ruinous victory, Normandy won, his enemies routed, and now everything swept aside, broken apart upon an obstinate rock, washed away in a malicious sea. His only lawful son, recently married in splendour, now denied even a coffin and a grave, for if ever they found those royal bodies it would be by the relenting grace of God, for the sea seldom put its winnings ashore by Barfleur. Even some of his unlawful sons, of whom there were many, gone down with their royal brother, no one left but the one legal daughter to inherit a barren empire.

Cadfael walked alone in a corner of the King's park and considered the foolishness of mortal vainglory, that was paid for with such a bitter price. But also he thought of the affairs of little men, to whom even a luckless King owed justice. For somewhere there was still to be sought the lost prior of Shrewsbury, carried off by masterless men in the forest, a litigant who might still be lost three days hence, when his suit came up again for hearing, unless someone in the meantime knew where to look for him.

He was in little doubt now. A lawless gang at liberty so close to a royal palace was in any case unlikely enough, and Cadfael was liable to brood on the unlikely. But that there should be two—no, that was impossible. And if one only, then that same one whose ambush he had overheard at some distance, yet close enough, too close for comfort, to Roger Mauduit's hunting-lodge.

Probably the unhappy brothers from Shrewsbury were off beating the wilds of the forest afresh. Cadfael knew better where to look. No doubt Roger was biting his nails in some anxiety over the delay, but he had no reason to suppose that three days would release the captive to appear against him, nor was he paying much attention to what his Welsh man-at-arms was doing with his time.

Cadfael took his horse and rode back without haste towards the hunting-lodge. He left in the early dusk, as soon as the evening meal was over in Mauduit's lodging. No one was paying any heed to him by that time of day. All Roger had to do was hold his tongue and keep his wits about him for three days, and the disputed manor would still be adjudged to him. Everything was beautifully in hand, after all.

Two of the men-at-arms and one groom had been left behind at the hunting-lodge. Cadfael doubted if the man they guarded was to be found in the house itself, for unless he was blindfolded he would be able to gather far too much knowledge of his surroundings, and the fable of the masterless men would be tossed into the rubbish-heap. No, he would be held in darkness, or dim light at best, even during the day, in straw or the rush flooring of a common hut, fed adequately but plainly and roughly, as wild men might keep a prisoner they were too cautious to kill, or too superstitious, until they turned him loose in some remote place, stripped of everything he had of value. On the other hand, he must be somewhere securely inside the boundary fence, otherwise there would be too high a risk of his being found. Between the gate and the house there were trees enough to obscure the large holding of a man of consequence. Somewhere among the stables and barns, or the now empty kennels, there he must be held.

Cadfael tethered his horse in cover well aside from the lodge and found himself a perch in a tall oak tree, from which vantage point he could see over the fence into the courtyard.

He was in luck. The three within fed themselves at leisure before they fed their prisoner, preferring to wait for dark. By the time the groom emerged from the hall with a pitcher and a bowl in his hands, Cadfael had his night eyes. They were quite easy about their charge, expecting no interference from any man. The groom vanished momentarily between the trees within the enclosure, but appeared again at one of the low buildings tucked under the fence, set down his pitcher for a moment while he hoisted clear a heavy wooden bar that held the door fast shut, and vanished within. The door thudded to after him, as though he had slammed it shut with his back braced against it, taking no chances even with an elderly monastic. In a few minutes he emerged again empty-handed, hauled the bar into place again, and returned, whistling, to the hall and the enjoyment of Mauduit's ale.

Not the stables nor the kennels, but a small, stout hay-store built on short wooden piles raised from the ground. At least the prior would have fairly snug lying.

Cadfael let the last of the light fade before he made a move. The wooden wall was stout and high, but more than one of the old trees outside leaned a branch over it, and it was no great labour to climb without and drop into the deep grass within. He made first for the gate, and quietly un-barred the narrow wicket set into it. Faint threads of torch-light filtered through the chinks in the hall shutters, but nothing else stirred. Cadfael laid hold of the heavy bar of the storehouse door, and eased it silently out of its socket, open-ing the door by cautious inches, and whispering through the chink: "Father. . . ?"

There was a sharp rustling of hay within, but no immedi-ate reply.

"Father Prior, is it you? Softly. . . . Are you bound?"

A hesitant and slightly timorous voice said: "No." And in a moment, with better assurance: "My son, you are not one of these sinful men?"

"Sinful man I am, but not of their company. Hush, quietly now! I have a horse close by. I came from Woodstock to find you. Reach me your hand, Father, and come forth."

A hand came wavering out of the hay-scented darkness to clutch convulsively at Cadfael's hand. The pale patch of a tonsured crown gleamed faintly, and a small, rounded figure crept forth and stepped into the thick grass. He had the wit to waste no breath then on questions, but stood docile and silent while Cadfael re-barred the door on emptiness, and, taking him by the hand, led him softly along the fence to the unfastened wicket in the great gate. Only when the door was closed as softly behind them did he heave a great, thankful sigh.

They were out, it was done, and no one would be likely to learn of the escape until morning. Cadfael led the way to where he had left his horse tethered. The forest lay serene and quiet about them.

"You ride, Father, and I'll walk with you. It's no more than two miles into Woodstock. We're safe enough now."

Bewildered and confused by so sudden a reversal, the prior confided and obeyed like a child. Not until they were out on the silent highroad did he say sadly, "I have failed of my mission. Son, may God bless you for this kindness which is beyond my understanding. For how did you know of me, and how could you divine where to find me? I understand nothing of what has been happening to me. And I am not a very brave man. . . . But my failure is no fault of yours, and my blessing I owe you without stint."

"You have not failed, Father," said Cadfael simply. "The suit is still unheard, and will be for three days more. All your companions are safe in Woodstock, except that they fret and search for you. And if you know where they will be lodging, I would recommend that you join them now, by night, and stay well out of sight until the day the case is heard. For if this trap was designed to keep you from appearing in the King's court, some further attempt might yet be made. Have you your evidences safe? They did not take them?"

"Brother Orderic, my clerk, was carrying the documents, but he could not conduct the case in court. I only am accredited to represent my abbot. But, my son, how is it that the case still goes unheard? The King keeps strict day and time, it's well known. How comes it that God and you have saved me from disgrace and loss?"

"Father, for all too bitter reason the King could not be present."

Cadfael told him the whole of it, how half the young chivalry of England had been wiped out in one blow, and the King left without an heir. Prior Heribert, shocked and dismayed, fell to praying in a grieving whisper for both dead and living, and Cadfael walked beside the horse in silence, for what more was there to be said? Except that King Henry, even in this shattering hour, willed that his justice should still prevail, and that was virtue in any monarch. Only when they came into the sleeping town did Cadfael again interrupt the prior's fervent prayers with a strange question.

"Father, was any man of your escort carrying steel? A dagger, or any such weapon?"

"No, no, God forbid!" said the prior, shocked. "We have no use for arms. We trust in God's peace, and after it in the King's."

"So I thought," said Cadfael, nodding. "It is another discipline, for another venture."

By the change in Mauduit's countenance Cadfael knew the hour of the following day when the news reached him that his prisoner was flown. All the rest of that day he went about with nerves at stretch and ears pricked for any sensational rumours being bandied around the town, and eyes roving anxiously in dread of the sight of Prior Heribert in court or street, braced to pour out his complaint to the King's officers. But as the hours passed and still there was no sign, he began to be a little eased in his mind, and to hope still for a miraculous deliverance. The Benedictine brothers were seen here and there, mute and sombre-faced; surely they could have had no word of their superior. There was nothing to be done but set his teeth, keep his countenance, wait and hope.

The second day passed, and the third day came, and Mauduit's hopes had soared again, for still there was no word. He made his appearance before the King's judge confidently, his charters in hand. The abbey was the suitor. If all went well, Roger would not even have to state his case, for the plea would fail of itself when the pleader failed to appear.

It came as a shattering shock when a sudden stir at the door, prompt to the hour appointed, blew into the hall a small, round, unimpressive person in the Benedictine habit, hugging to him an armful of vellum rolls, and followed by his black-gowned brothers in close attendance. Cadfael, too, was observing him with interest, for it was the first time he had seen him clearly. A modest man of comfortable figure and amiable countenance, rosy and mild. Not so old as that night journey had suggested, perhaps forty-five, with a shining innocence about him. But to Roger Mauduit it might have been a fire-breathing dragon entering the hall.

And who would have expected, from that gentle, even deprecating presence, the clarity and expertise with which that small man deployed his original charter, punctiliously identical to Roger's, according to the account Alard had given, and omitting any specific mention of what should follow Arnulf Mauduit's death—how scrupulously he pointed out the omission and the arguments to which it might give rise, and followed it up with two letters written by that same

Arnulf Mauduit to Abbot Fulchered, referring in plain terms to the obligatory return of the manor and village after his death, and pledging his son's loyal observance of the obligation.

It might have been want of proofs that caused Roger to make so poor a job of refuting the evidence, or it might have been craven conscience. Whatever the cause, judgement was given for the abbey.

Cadfael presented himself before the lord. He was leaving barely an hour after the verdict was given.

"My lord, your suit is concluded, and my service with it. I have done what I pledged, here I part from you."

Roger sat sunk in gloom and rage, and lifted upon him a glare that should have felled him, but failed of its impact.

"I misdoubt me," said Roger, smouldering, "how you have observed your loyalty to me. Who else could know. . . ?" He bit his tongue in time, for as long as it remained unsaid no accusation had been made, and no rebuttal was needed. He would have liked to ask: How *did* you know? But he thought better of it. "Go, then, if you have nothing more to say."

"As to that," said Cadfael meaningly, "nothing more need be said. It's over." And that was recognisable as a promise, but with uneasy implications, for plainly on some other matter he still had a thing to say.

"My lord, give some thought to this, for I was until now in your service, and wish you no harm. Of those four who attended Prior Heribert on his way here, not one carried arms. There was neither sword nor dagger nor knife of any kind among the five of them."

He saw the significance of that go home, slowly but with

bitter force. The masterless men had been nothing but a children's tale, but until now Roger had thought, as he had been meant to think, that that dagger-stroke in the forest had been a bold attempt by an abbey servant to defend his prior. He blinked and swallowed and stared, and began to sweat, beholding a perilous gulf into which he had all but stumbled.

"There were none there who bore arms," said Cadfael, "but your own."

A double-edged ambush that had been, to have him out in the forest by night, all unsuspecting. And there were as many miles between Woodstock and Sutton Mauduit returning as coming, and there would be other nights as dark on the way.

"Who?" asked Roger in a grating whisper. "Which of them? Give him a name!"

"No," said Cadfael simply. "Do your own divining. I am no longer in your service, I have said all I mean to say."

Roger's face had turned grey. He was hearing again the plan unfolded so seductively in his ear. "You cannot leave me so! If you know so much, for God's sake return with me, see me safely home, at least. You I could trust!"

"No," said Cadfael again. "You are warned, now guard yourself."

It was fair, he considered; it was enough. He turned and went away without another word. He went, just as he was, to Vespers in the parish church, for no better reason—or so he thought then—than that the dimness within the open doorway beckoned him as he turned his back on a duty completed, inviting him to quietness and thought, and the bell was just sounding. The little prior was there, ardent in thanksgiving, one more creature who had fumbled his way to the completion of a task, and the turning of a leaf in the book of his life.

Cadfael watched out the office, and stood mute and still for some time after priest and worshippers had departed. The silence after their going was deeper than the ocean and more secure than the earth. Cadfael breathed and consumed it like new bread. It was the light touch of a small hand on the hilt of his sword that startled him out of that profound isolation. He looked down to see a little acolyte, no higher than his elbow, regarding him gravely from great round eyes of blinding blue, intent and challenging, as solemn as ever was angelic messenger.

"Sir," said the child in stern treble reproof, tapping the hilt with an infant finger, "should not all weapons of war be laid aside here?"

"Sir," said Cadfael hardly less gravely, though he was smiling, "you may very well be right." And slowly he unbuckled the sword from his belt, and went and laid it down, flatlings, on the lowest step under the altar. It looked strangely appropriate and at peace there. The hilt, after all, was a cross.

Prior Heribert was at a frugal supper with his happy brothers in the parish priest's house when Cadfael asked audience with him. The little man came out graciously to welcome a stranger, and knew him for an acquaintance at least, and now at a breath certainly a friend.

"You, my son! And surely it was you at Vespers? I felt that I should know the shape of you. You are the most welcome of guests here, and if there is anything I and mine can do to repay you for what you did for us, you need but name it."

"Father," said Cadfael, briskly Welsh in his asking, "do you ride for home tomorrow?"

"Surely, my son, we leave after Prime. Abbot Godefrid will be waiting to hear how we have fared."

"Then, Father, here am I at the turning of my life, free of one master's service, and finished with arms. Take me with you!"

The
Price
of Light

amo FitzHamon of Lidyate held two fat manors in the north-eastern corner of the county, towards the border of Cheshire. Though a gross feeder, a heavy drinker, a self-indulgent lecher, a harsh land-lord and a brutal master, he had reached the age of sixty in the best of health, and it came as a salutary shock to him when he was at last taken with a mild seizure, and for the first time in his life saw the next world yawning before him, and woke to the uneasy consciousness that it might see fit to treat him somewhat more austerely than this world had done. Though he repented none of them, he was aware of a whole register of acts in his past which heaven might construe as heavy sins. It began to seem to him a prudent precaution to acquire merit for his soul as quickly as possible. Also as cheaply, for he was a grasping and possessive man. **45**

A judicious gift to some holy house should secure the
welfare of his soul. There was no need to go so far as
endowing an abbey, or a new church of his own. The
Benedictine abbey of Shrewsbury could put up a powerful
assault of prayers on his behalf in return for a much more
modest gift.

The thought of alms to the poor, however ostentatiously
bestowed in the first place, did not recommend itself.
Whatever was given would be soon consumed and forgotten, and a rag-tag of beggarly blessings from the indigent
could carry very little weight, besides failing to confer a
lasting lustre upon himself. No, he wanted something that
would continue in daily use and daily respectful notice, a
permanent reminder of his munificence and piety. He took
his time about making his decision, and when he was
satisfied of the best value he could get for the least expen-
diture, he sent his law-man to Shrewsbury to confer with
abbot and prior, and conclude with due ceremony and many
witnesses the charter that conveyed to the custodian of the
altar of St. Mary, within the abbey church, one of his free
tenant farmers, the rent to provide light for Our Lady's altar
throughout the year. He promised also, for the proper
displaying of his charity, the gift of a pair of fine silver
candlesticks, which he himself would bring and see installed
on the altar at the coming Christmas feast.

Abbot Heribert, who after a long life of repeated disillusionments still contrived to think the best of everybody, was
moved to tears by this penitential generosity. Prior Robert,
himself an aristocrat, refrained, out of Norman solidarity,
from casting doubt upon Hamo's motive, but he elevated his
eyebrows, all the same. Brother Cadfael, who knew only the
public reputation of the donor, and was sceptical enough to
suspend judgement until he encountered the source, said

nothing, and waited to observe and decide for himself. Not
that he expected much; he had been in the world fifty-five
years, and learned to temper all his expectations, bad or
good.

It was with mild and detached interest that he observed
the arrival of the party from Lidyate, on the morning of
Christmas Eve. A hard, cold Christmas it was proving to be,
that year of 1135, all bitter black frost and grudging snow,
thin and sharp as whips before a withering east wind. The
weather had been vicious all the year, and the harvest a
disaster. In the villages people shivered and starved, and
Brother Oswalk the almoner fretted and grieved the more
that the alms he had to distribute were not enough to keep
all those bodies and souls together. The sight of a cavalcade
of three good riding horses, ridden by travelers richly
wrapped up from the cold, and followed by two pack-
ponies, brought all the wretched petitioners crowding and
crying, holding out hands blue with frost. All they got out of
it was a single perfunctory handful of small coin, and when
they hampered his movements FitzHamon used his whip as
a matter of course to clear the way. Rumour, thought Brother
Cadfael, pausing on his way to the infirmary with his daily
medicines for the sick, had probably not done Hamo FitzHamon any injustice.

Dismounting in the greater court, the knight of Lidyate
was seen to be a big, over-fleshed, top-heavy man with
bushy hair and beard and eyebrows, all grey-streaked from
their former black, and stiff and bristling as wire. He might
well have been a very handsome man before indulgence
purpled his face and pocked his skin and sank his sharp
black eyes deep into flabby sacks of flesh. He looked more
than his age, but still a man to be reckoned with.

The second horse carried his lady, pillion behind a groom.
A small figure she made, even swathed almost to invisibility
in her woollens and furs, and she rode snuggled comfortably
against the groom's broad back, her arms hugging him
round the waist. And a very well-looking young fellow he
was, this groom, a strapping lad barely twenty years old,
with ruddy cheeks and merry, guileless eyes, long in the
legs, wide in the shoulders, everything a country youth
should be, and attentive to his duties into the bargain, for he
was down from the saddle in one lithe leap, and reaching up
to take the lady by the waist, every bit as heartily as she had
been clasping him a moment before, and lift her lightly
down. Small, gloved hands rested on his shoulders a brief
moment longer than necessary. His respectful support of her
continued until she was safe on the ground and sure of her
footing; perhaps a few seconds more. Hamo FitzHamon was
occupied with Prior Robert's ceremonious welcome, and the
attentions of the hospitaller, who had made the best rooms
of the guest-hall ready for him.

The third horse also carried two people, but the woman on
the pillion did not wait for anyone to help her down, but slid
quickly to the ground and hurried to help her mistress off
with the great outer cloak in which she had travelled. A
quiet, submissive young woman, perhaps in her middle
twenties, perhaps older, in drab homespun, her hair hidden
away under a coarse linen wimple. Her face was thin and
pale, her skin dazzlingly fair, and her eyes, reserved and
weary, were of a pale, clear blue, a fierce colour that ill suited
their humility and resignation.

Lifting the heavy folds from her lady's shoulders, the maid
showed a head the taller of the two, but drab indeed beside
the bright little bird that emerged from the cloak. Lady

FitzHamon came forth graciously smiling on the world in scarlet and brown, like a robin, and just as confidently. She had dark hair braided about a small, shapely head, soft, full cheeks flushed rosy by the chill air, and large dark eyes assured of their charm and power. She could not possibly have been more than thirty, probably not so much. FitzHamon had a grown son somewhere, with children of his own, and waiting, some said with little patience, for his inheritance. This girl must be a second or third wife, a good deal younger than her stepson, and a beauty, at that. Hamo was secure enough and important enough to keep himself supplied with wives as he wore them out. This one must have cost him dear, for she had not the air of a poor but pretty relative sold for a profitable alliance; rather she looked as if she knew her own status very well indeed, and meant to have it acknowledged. She would look well presiding over the high table at Lidyate, certainly, which was probably the main consideration.

The groom behind whom the maid had ridden was an older man, lean and wiry, with a face like the bole of a knotty oak. By the sardonic patience of his eyes he had been in close and relatively favoured attendance on FitzHamon for many years, knew the best and the worst his moods could do, and was sure of his own ability to ride the storms. Without a word he set about unloading the pack-horses, and followed his lord to the guest-hall, while the young man took FitzHamon's bridle, and led the horses away to the stables.

Cadfael watched the two women cross to the doorway, the lady springy as a young hind, with bright eyes taking in everything around her, the tall maid keeping always a pace behind, with long steps curbed to keep her distance. Even thus, frustrated like a mewed hawk, she had a graceful gait.

Almost certainly of villein stock, like the two grooms. Cadfael had long practice in distinguishing the free from the unfree. Not that the free had any easy life, often they were worse off than the villeins of their neighbourhood; there were plenty of free men, this Christmas, gaunt and hungry, forced to hold out begging hands among the throng round the gatehouse. Freedom, the first ambition of every man, still could not fill the bellies of wives and children in a bad season.

FitzHamon and his party appeared at Vespers in full glory, to see the candlesticks reverently installed upon the altar in the Lady Chapel. Abbot, prior and brothers had no difficulty in sufficiently admiring the gift, for they were indeed things of beauty, two fluted stems ending in the twin cups of flowering lilies. Even the veins of the leaves showed delicate and perfect as in the living plant. Brother Oswald the almoner, himself a skilled silversmith when he had time to exercise his craft, stood gazing at the new embellishments of the altar with a face and mind curiously torn between rapture and regret, and ventured to delay the donor for a moment, as he was being ushered away to sup with Abbot Heribert in his lodging.

"My lord, these are of truly noble workmanship. I have some knowledge of precious metals, and of the most notable craftsmen in these parts, but I never saw any work so true to the plant as this. A countryman's eye is here, but the hand of a court craftsman. May we know who made them?"

FitzHamon's marred face curdled into deeper purple, as if an unpardonable shadow had been cast upon his hour of self-congratulation. He said brusquely: "I commissioned them from a fellow in my own service. You would not know his name—a villein born, but he had some skill." And with that he swept on, avoiding further question, and wife and men-servants and maid trailed after him. Only the older groom, who seemed less in awe of his lord than anyone, perhaps by reason of having so often presided over the ceremony of carrying him dead-drunk to his bed, turned back for a moment to pluck at Brother Oswald's sleeve, and advise him in a confidential whisper: "You'll find him short to question on that head. The silversmith—Alard, his name was—cut and ran from his service last Christmas, and for all they hunted him as far as London, where the signs pointed, he's never been found. I'd let that matter lie, if I were you."

And with that he trotted away after his master, and left several thoughtful faces staring after him.

"Not a man to part willingly with any property of his," mused Brother Cadfael, "metal or man, but for a price, and a steep price at that."

"Brother, be ashamed!" reproved Brother Jerome at his elbow. "Has he not parted with these very treasures from pure charity?"

Cadfael refrained from elaborating on the profit FitzHamon expected for his benevolence. It was never worth arguing with Jerome, who in any case knew as well as anyone that the silver lilies and the rent of one farm were no free gift. But Brother Oswald said grievingly: "I wish he had directed his charity better. Surely these are beautiful things, a delight to the eyes, but well sold, they could have provided money enough to buy the means of keeping my poorest petitioners alive through the winter, some of whom will surely die for the want of them."

Brother Jerome was scandalized. "Has he not given them to Our Lady herself?" he lamented indignantly. "Beware of the sin of those apostles who cried out with the same complaint against the woman who brought the pot of spikenard, and poured it over the Saviour's feet. Remember Our Lord's reproof to them, that they should let her alone, for she had done well!"

"Our Lord was acknowledging a well-meant impulse of devotion," said Brother Oswald with spirit. "He did not say it was well advised! 'She hath done what she could' is what he said. He never said that with a little thought she might not have done better. What use would it have been to wound the giver, after the thing was done? Spilled oil of spikenard could hardly be recovered."

His eyes dwelt with love and compunction upon the silver lilies, with their tall stems of wax and flame. For these remained, and to divert them to other use was still possible, or would have been possible if the donor had been a more approachable man. He had, after all, a right to dispose as he wished of his own property.

"It is sin," admonished Jerome sanctimoniously, "even to covet for other use, however worthy, that which has been given to Our lady. The very thought is sin."

"If Our Lady could make her own will known," said Brother Cadfael drily, "we might learn which is the graver sin, and which the more acceptable sacrifice."

"Could any price be too high for the lighting of this holy altar?" demanded Jerome.

It was a good question, Cadfael thought, as they went to supper in the refectory. Ask Brother Jordan, for instance, the value of light. Jordan was old and frail, and gradually going blind. As yet he could distinguish shapes, but like shadows in a dream, though he knew his way about the cloisters and precincts so well that his gathering darkness was no hindrance to his freedom of movement. But as every day the twilight closed in on him by a shade, so did his profound love of light grow daily more devoted, until he had forsaken other duties, and taken upon himself to tend all the lamps and candles on both altars, for the sake of being always irradiated by light, and sacred light, at that. As soon as Compline was over, this evening, he would be busy devoutly trimming the wicks of candle and lamp, to have the steady flames smokeless and immaculate for the Matins of Christmas Day. Doubtful if he would go to his bed at all until Matins and Lauds were over. The very old need little sleep, and sleep is itself a kind of darkness. But what Jordan treasured was the flame of light, and not the vessel holding it; and would not those splendid two-pound candles shine upon him just as well from plain wooden sconces?

Cadfael was in the warming-house with the rest of the brothers, about a quarter of an hour before Compline, when a lay brother from the guest-hall came enquiring for him.

"The lady asks if you'll speak with her. She's complaining of a bad head, and that she'll never be able to sleep. Brother Hospitaller recommended her to you for a remedy."

Cadfael went with him without comment, but with some curiosity, for at Vespers the Lady FitzHamon had looked in blooming health and sparkling spirits. Nor did she seem greatly changed when he met her in the hall, though she was still swathed in the cloak she had worn to cross the great court to and from the abbot's house, and had the hood so drawn that it shadowed her face. The silent maid hovered at her shoulder.

"You are Brother Cadfael? They tell me you are expert in herbs and medicines, and can certainly help me. I came early back from the lord abbot's supper, with such a headache, and have told my lord that I shall go early to bed. But I have such disturbed sleep, and with this pain how shall I be able to rest? Can you give me some draught that will ease me? They say you have a perfect apothecarium in your herb garden, and all your own work, growing, gathering, drying, brewing and all. There must be something there that can soothe pain and bring deep sleep."

Well, thought Cadfael, small blame to her if she sometimes sought a means to ward off her old husband's rough attentions for a night, especially for a festival night when he was likely to have drunk heavily. Nor was it Cadfael's business to question whether the petitioner really needed his remedies. A guest might ask for whatever the house afforded.

"I have a syrup of my own making," he said, "which may do you good service. I'll bring you a vial of it from my workshop store."

"May I come with you? I should like to see your workshop." She had forgotten to sound frail and tired, the voice could have been a curious child's. "As I already am cloaked and shod," she said winningly. "We just returned from the lord abbot's table."

"But should you not go in from the cold, madam? Though the snow's swept here in the court, it lies on some of the garden paths."

"A few minutes in the fresh air will help me," she said, "before trying to sleep. And it cannot be far."

It was not far. Once away from the subdued lights of the buildings they were aware of the stars, snapping like sparks from a cold fire, in a clear black sky just engendering a few tattered snow-clouds in the east. In the garden, between the pleached hedges, it seemed almost warm, as though the sleeping trees breathed tempered air as well as cutting off the bleak wind. The silence was profound. The herb garden was walled, and the wooden hut where Cadfael brewed and stored his medicines was sheltered from the worst of the cold. Once inside, and a small lamp kindled, Lady FitzHamon forgot her invalid role in wonder and delight, looking round her with bright, inquisitive eyes. The maid, submissive and still, scarcely turned her head, but her eyes ranged from left to right, and a faint colour touched life into her cheeks. The many faint, sweet scents made her nostrils quiver, and her lips curve just perceptibly with pleasure.

Curious as a cat, the lady probed into every sack and jar and box, peered at mortars and bottles, and asked a hundred questions in a breath.

"And this is rosemary, these little dried needles? And in this great sack—is it grain?" She plunged her hands wrist-deep inside the neck of it, and the hut was filled with sweetness. "Lavender? Such a great harvest of it? Do you, then, prepare perfumes for us women?"

"Lavender has other good properties," said Cadfael. He was filling a small vial with a clear syrup he made from eastern poppies, a legacy of his crusading years. "It is helpful for all disorders that trouble the head and spirit, and its scent is calming. I'll give you a little pillow filled with that and other herbs, that shall help to bring you sleep. But this draught will ensure it. You may take all that I give you here, and get no harm, only a good night's rest."

She had been playing inquisitively with a pile of small clay dishes he kept by his work-bench, rough dishes in which the fine seeds sifted from fruiting plants could be spread to dry out; but she came at once to gaze eagerly at the modest vial he presented to her. "Is it enough? It takes much to give me sleep."

"This," he assured her patiently, "would bring sleep to a strong man. But it will not harm even a delicate lady like you."

She took it in her hand with a small, sleek smile of satisfaction. "Then I thank you indeed! I will make a gift—shall I?—to your almoner in requital. Elfgiva, you bring the little pillow. I shall breathe it all night long. It should sweeten dreams."

So her name was Elfgiva. A Norse name. She had Norse eyes, as he had already noted, blue as ice, and pale, fine skin worn finer and whiter by weariness. All this time she had noted everything that passed, motionless, and never said a word. Was she older, or younger, than her lady? There was no guessing. The one was so clamant, and the other so still.

He put out his lamp and closed the door, and led them back to the great court just in time to take leave of them and still be prompt for Compline. Clearly the lady had no intention of attending. As for the lord, he was just being helped away from the abbot's lodging, his grooms supporting him one on either side, though as yet he was not gravely drunk. They headed for the guest-hall at an easy roll. No doubt only the hour of Compline had concluded the drawn-out supper, probably to the abbot's considerable relief. He was no drinker, and could have very little in common with Hamo FitzHamon. Apart, of course, from a deep devotion to the altar of St. Mary.

The lady and her maid had already vanished within the guest-hall. The younger groom carried in his free hand a large jug, full, to judge by the way he held it. The young wife could drain her draught and clutch her herbal pillow with confidence; the drinking was not yet at an end, and her sleep would be solitary and untroubled. Brother Cadfael went to Compline mildly sad, and obscurely comforted.

Only when service was ended, and the brothers on the way to their beds, did he remember that he had left his flask of poppy syrup unstoppered. Not that it would come to any harm in the frosty night, but his sense of fitness drove him to go and remedy the omission before he slept.

His sandalled feet, muffled in strips of woollen cloth for warmth and safety on the frozen paths, made his coming quite silent, and he was already reaching out a hand to the latch of the door, but not yet touching, when he was brought up short and still by the murmur of voices within. Soft, whispering, dreamy voices that made sounds less and more than speech, caresses rather than words, though once at least words surfaced for a moment. A man's voice, young, wary, saying: "But how if he *does*. . . ?" And a woman's soft, suppressed laughter: "He'll sleep till morning, never fear!" And her words were suddenly hushed with kissing, and her laughter became huge, ecstatic sighs; the young man's breath heaving triumphantly, but still, a moment later, the note of fear again, half-enjoyed: "Still, you know him, he *may* . . ." And she, soothing: "Not for an hour, at least . . . then we'll go . . . it will grow cold here. . . ."

That, at any rate, was true; small fear of them wishing to sleep out the night here, even two close-wrapped in one cloak on the bench-bed against the wooden wall. Brother Cadfael withdrew very circumspectly from the herb garden, and made his way back in chastened thought towards the dortoir. Now he knew who had swallowed that draught of his, and it was not the lady. In the pitcher of wine the young groom had been carrying? Enough for a strong man, even if he had not been drunk already. Meantime, no doubt, the body-servant was left to put his lord to bed, somewhere apart from the chamber where the lady lay supposedly nursing her indisposition and sleeping the sleep of the innocent. Ah, well, it was no business of Cadfael's, nor had he any intention of getting involved. He did not feel particularly censorious. Doubtful if she ever had any choice about marrying Hamo; and with this handsome boy for ever about them, to point the contrast . . . A brief experience of genuine passion, echoing old loves, pricked sharply through the years of his vocation. At least he knew what he was condoning. And who could help feeling some admiration for her opportunist daring, the quick wit that had procured the means, the alert eye that had seized on the most remote and adequate shelter available?

Cadfael went to bed, and slept without dreams, and rose at the Matins bell, some minutes before midnight. The procession of the brothers wound its way down the night stairs into the church, and into the soft, full glow of the lights before St. Mary's altar.

Withdrawn reverently some yards from the step of the altar, old Brother Jordan, who should long ago have been in his cell with the rest, kneeled upright with clasped hands and ecstatic face, in which the great, veiled eyes stared full into the light he loved. When Prior Robert exclaimed in concern at finding him there on the stones, and laid a hand on his shoulder, he started as if out of a trance, and lifted to them a countenance itself all light.

"Oh, brothers, I have been so blessed! I have lived through a wonder. . . . Praise God that ever it was granted to me! But bear with me, for I am forbidden to speak of it to any, for three days. On the third day from today I may speak. . . !"

"Look, brothers!" wailed Jerome suddenly, pointing. "Look at the altar!"

Every man present, except Jordan, who still serenely prayed and smiled, turned to gape where Jerome pointed. The tall candles stood secured by drops of their own wax in two small clay dishes, such as Cadfael used for sorting seeds. The two silver lilies were gone from the place of honour.

Through loss, disorder, consternation and suspicion, Prior Robert would still hold fast to the order of the day. Let Hamo FitzHamon sleep in happy ignorance till morning, still Matins and Lauds must be properly celebrated. Christmas was larger than all the giving and losing of silverware. Grimly he saw the services of the church observed, and despatched the brethren back to their beds until Prime, to sleep or lie wakeful and fearful, as they might. Nor would he allow any pestering of Brother Jordan by others, though possibly he did try in private to extort something more satisfactory from the old man. Clearly the theft, whether he knew anything about it or not, troubled Jordan not at all. To everything he said only: "I am enjoined to silence until midnight of the third day." And when they asked by whom? he smiled seraphically, and was silent.

It was Robert himself who broke the news to Hamo Fitz-Hamon, in the morning, before Mass. The uproar, though vicious, was somewhat tempered by the after-effects of Cadfael's poppy draught, which dulled the edges of energy, if not of malice. His body-servant, the older groom Sweyn, was keeping well back out of reach, even with Robert still present, and the lady sat somewhat apart, too, as though still frail and possibly a little out of temper. She exclaimed dutifully, and apparently sincerely, at the outrage done to her husband, and echoed his demand that the thief should be hunted down, and the candlesticks recovered. Prior Robert was just as zealous in the matter. No effort should be spared to regain the princely gift, of that they could be sure. He had already made certain of various circumstances which should limit the hunt. There had been a brief fall of snow after Compline, just enough to lay down a clean film of white on the ground. No single footprint had as yet marked this pure layer. He had only to look for himself at the paths leading from both parish doors of the church to see that no one had left by that way. The porter would swear that no one had passed the gatehouse; and on the one side of the abbey grounds not walled, the Meole brook was full and frozen, but the snow on both sides of it was virgin. Within the enclave, of course, tracks and cross-tracks were trodden out everywhere; but no one had left the enclave since Compline, when the candlesticks were still in their place.

"So the miscreant is still within the walls?" said Hamo, glinting vengefully. "So much the better! Then his booty is still here within, too, and if we have to turn all your abode doors out of dortoirs, we'll find it! It, and him!"

"We will search everywhere," agreed Robert, "and question every man. We are as deeply offended as your lordship at this blasphemous crime. You may yourself oversee the search, if you will."

So all that Christmas Day, alongside the solemn rejoicings in the church, an angry hunt raged about the precincts in full cry. It was not difficult for all the monks to account for their time to the last minute, their routine being so ordered that brother inevitably extricated brother from suspicion; and such as had special duties that took them out of the general view, like Cadfael in his visit to the herb garden, had all

witnesses to vouch for them. The lay brothers ranged more freely, but tended to work in pairs, at least. The servants and the few guests protested their innocence, and if they had not, all of them, others willing to prove it, neither could Hamo prove the contrary. When it came to his own two grooms, there were several witnesses to testify that Sweyn had returned to his bed in the lofts of the stables as soon as he had put his lord to bed, and certainly empty-handed; and Sweyn, as Cadfael noted with interest, swore unblinkingly that young Madoc, who had come in an hour after him, had none the less returned with him, and spent that hour, at Sweyn's order, tending one of the pack-ponies, which showed signs of a cough, and that otherwise they had been together throughout.

A villein instinctively closing ranks with his kind against his lord? wondered Cadfael. Or does Sweyn know very well where that young man was last night, or at least what he was about, and is he intent on protecting him from a worse vengeance? No wonder Madoc looked a shade less merry and ruddy than usual this morning, though on the whole he kept his countenance very well, and refrained from even looking at the lady, while her tone to him was cool, sharp and distant.

Cadfael left them hard at it again after the miserable meal they made of dinner, and went into the church alone. While they were feverishly searching every corner for the candlesticks he had forborne from taking part, but now they were elsewhere he might find something of interest there. He would not be looking for anything so obvious as two large silver candlesticks. He made obeisance at the altar, and mounted the step to look closely at the burning candles. No one had paid any attention to the modest containers that had been substituted for Hamo's gift, and just as well, in their circumstances, that Cadfael's workshop was very little visited, or these little clay pots might have been recognized as coming from there. He moulded and baked them himself as he wanted them. He had no intention of condoning theft, but neither did he relish the idea of any creature, however sinful, falling into Hamo FitzHamon's mercies.

Something long and fine, a thread of silver-gold, was caught and coiled in the wax at the base of one candle. Carefully he detached candle from holder, and unlaced from it a long, pale hair; to make sure of retaining it, he broke off the imprisoning disc of wax with it, and then hoisted and turned the candle to see if anything else was to be found under it. One tiny oval dot showed; with a fingernail he extracted a single seed of lavender. Left in the dish from beforetime? He thought not. The stacked pots were all empty. No, this had been brought here in the fold of a sleeve, most probably, and shaken out while the candle was being transferred.

The lady had plunged both hands with pleasure into the sack of lavender, and moved freely about his workshop investigating everything. It would have been easy to take two of these dishes unseen, and wrap them in a fold of her cloak. Even more plausible, she might have delegated the task to young Madoc, when they crept away from their assignation. Supposing, say, they had reached the desperate point of planning flight together, and needed funds to set them on their way to some safe refuge . . . yes, there were possibilities. In the meantime, the grain of lavender had given Cadfael another idea. And there was, of course, that long, fine hair, pale as flax, but brighter. The boy was fair. But so fair?

He went out through the frozen garden to his herbarium, shut himself securely into his workshop, and opened the sack of lavender, plunging both arms to the elbow and groping through the chill, smooth sweetness that parted and slid like grain. They were there, well down, his fingers traced the shape first of one, then a second. He sat down to consider what must be done.

Finding the lost valuables did not identify the thief. He could produce and restore them at once, but FitzHamon would certainly pursue the hunt vindictively until he found the culprit; and Cadfael had seen enough of him to know that it might cost life and all before this complainant was satisfied. He needed to know more before he would hand over any man to be done to death. Better not leave the things here, however. He doubted if they would ransack his hut, but they might. He rolled the candlesticks in a piece of sacking, and thrust them into the centre of the pleached hedge where it was thickest. The meagre, frozen snow had dropped with the brief sun. His arm went in to the shoulder, and when he withdrew it, the twigs sprang back and covered all, holding the package securely. Whoever had first hidden it would surely come by night to reclaim it, and show a human face at last.

It was well that he had moved it, for the searchers, driven by an increasingly angry Hamo, reached his hut before Vespers, examined everything within it, while he stood by to prevent actual damage to his medicines, and went away satisfied that what they were seeking was not there. They had not, in fact, been very thorough about the sack of lavender, the candlesticks might well have escaped notice even if he had left them there. It did not occur to anyone to tear the hedges apart, luckily. When they were gone, to probe all the fodder and grain in the barns, Cadfael restored the silver to its original place. Let the bait lie safe in the trap until the quarry came to claim it, as he surely would, once relieved of the fear that the hunters might find it first.

Cadfael kept watch that night. He had no difficulty in absenting himself from the dortoir, once everyone was in bed and asleep. His cell was by the night stairs, and the prior slept at the far end of the long room, and slept deeply. And bitter though the night air was, the sheltered hut was barely colder than his cell, and he kept blankets there for swathing some of his jars and bottles against frost. He took his little box with tinder and flint, and hid himself in the corner behind the door. It might be a wasted vigil; the thief, having survived one day, might think it politic to venture yet another before removing his spoils.

But it was not wasted. He reckoned it might be as late as ten o'clock when he heard a light hand at the door. Two hours before the bell would sound for Matins, almost two hours since the household had retired. Even the guest-hall should be silent and asleep by now; the hour was carefully chosen. Cadfael held his breath, and waited. The door swung open, a shadow stole past him, light steps felt their way unerringly to where the sack of lavender was propped against the wall. Equally silently Cadfael swung the door to again, and set his back against it. Only then did he strike a spark, and hold the blown flame to the wick of his little lamp.

She did not start or cry out, or try to rush past him and escape into the night. The attempt would not have succeeded, and she had had long practice in enduring what could not be cured. She stood facing him as the small flame steadied and burned taller, her face shadowed by the hood of her cloak, the candlesticks clasped possessively to her breast.

"Elfgiva!" said Brother Cadfael gently. And then: "Are you here for yourself, or for your mistress?" But he thought he knew the answer already. That frivolous young wife would never really leave her rich husband and easy life, however tedious and unpleasant Hamo's attentions might be, to risk everything with her penniless villein lover. She would only keep him to enjoy in secret whenever she felt it safe. Even when the old man died she would submit to marriage at an overlord's will to another equally distasteful. She was not the stuff of which heroines and adventurers are made. This was another kind of woman.

Cadfael went close, and lifted a hand gently to put back the hood from her head. She was tall, a hand's-breadth taller than he, and erect as one of the lilies she clasped. The net that had covered her hair was drawn off with the hood, and a great flood of silver-gold streamed about her in the dim light, framing the pale face and startling blue eyes. Norse hair! The Danes had left their seed as far south as Cheshire, and planted this tall flower among them. She was no longer plain, tired and resigned. In this dim but loving light she shone in austere beauty. Just so must Brother Jordan's veiled eyes have seen her.

"Now I see!" said Cadfael. "You came into the Lady Chapel, and shone upon our half-blind brother's darkness as you shine here. You are the visitation that brought him awe and bliss, and enjoined silence upon him for three days."

The voice he had scarcely heard speak a word until then, a voice level, low, and beautiful, said: "I made no claim to be what I am not. It was he who mistook me. I did not refuse the gift."

"I understand. You had not thought to find anyone there, he took you by surprise as you took him. He took you for Our Lady herself, disposing as she saw fit of what had been given her. And you made him promise you three days' grace." The lady had plunged her hands into the sack, yes, but Elfgiva had carried the pillow, and a grain or two had filtered through the muslin to betray her.

"Yes," she said, watching him with unwavering blue eyes.

"So in the end you had nothing against him making known how the candlesticks were stolen." It was not an accusation, he was pursuing his way to understanding.

But at once she said clearly: "I did not steal them. I took them. I will restore them—to their owner."

"Then you don't claim they are yours?"

"No," she said, "they are not mine. But neither are they FitzHamon's."

"Do you tell me," said Cadfael mildly, "that there has been no theft at all?"

"Oh, yes," said Elfgiva, and her pallor burned into a fierce brightness, and her voice vibrated like a harp-string. "Yes, there has been a theft, and a vile, cruel theft, too, but not here, not now. The theft was a year ago, when FitzHamon received these candlesticks from Alard who made them, his villein, like me. Do you know what the promised price was for these? Manumission for Alard, and marriage with me, what we had begged of him three years and more. Even in villeinage we would have married and been thankful. But he promised freedom! Free man makes free wife, and I was promised, too. But when he got the fine works he wanted, then he refused the promised price. He laughed! I saw, I heard him! He kicked Alard away from him like a dog. So what was his due, and denied him, Alard took. He ran! On St. Stephen's Day he ran!"

"And left you behind?" said Cadfael gently.

"What chance had he to take me? Or even to bid me farewell? He was thrust out to manual labour on FitzHamon's other manor. When his chance came, he took it and fled. I was not sad! I rejoiced! Whether I live or die, whether he remembers or forgets me, he is free. No, but in two days more he will be free. For a year and a day he will have been working for his living in his own craft, in a charter borough, and after that he cannot be haled back into servitude, even if they find him."

"I do not think," said Brother Cadfael, "that he will have forgotten you! Now I see why our brother may speak after three days. It will be too late then to try to reclaim a runaway serf. And you hold that these exquisite things you are cradling belong by right to Alard who made them?"

"Surely," she said, "seeing he never was paid for them, they are still his."

"And you are setting out tonight to take them to him. Yes! As I heard it, they had some cause to pursue him towards London . . . indeed, into London, though they never found him. Have you had better word of him? *From* him?"

The pale face smiled. "Neither he nor I can read or write. And whom should he trust to carry word until his time is complete, and he is free? No, never any word."

"But Shrewsbury is also a charter borough, where the unfree may work their way to freedom in a year and a day. And sensible boroughs encourage the coming of good craftsmen, and will go far to hide and protect them. I know! So you think he may be here. And the trail towards London a false trail. True, why should he run so far, when there's help so near? But, daughter, what if you do not find him in Shrewsbury?"

"Then I will look for him elsewhere until I do. I can live as a runaway, too, I have skills, I can make my own way until I do get word of him. Shrewsbury can as well make room for a good seamstress as for a man's gifts, and someone in the silversmith's craft will know where to find a brother so talented as Alard. I shall find him!"

"And when you do? Oh, child, have you looked beyond that?"

"To the very end," said Elfgiva firmly. "If I find him and he no longer wants me, no longer thinks of me, if he is married and has put me out of his mind, then I will deliver him these things that belong to him, to do with as he pleases, and go my own way and make my own life as best I may without him. And wish well to him as long as I live."

Oh, no, small fear, she would not be easily forgotten, not in a year, not in many years. "And if he is utterly glad of you, and loves you still?"

"Then," she said, gravely smiling, "if he is of the same mind as I, I have made a vow to Our Lady, who lent me her semblance in the old man's eyes, that we will sell these candlesticks where they may fetch their proper price, and that price shall be delivered to your almoner to feed the hungry. And that will be our gift, Alard's and mine, though no one will ever know it."

"Our Lady will know it," said Cadfael, "and so shall I. Now, how were you planning to get out of this enclave and into Shrewsbury? Both our gates and the town gates are closed until morning."

She lifted eloquent shoulders. "The parish doors are not

barred. And even if I leave tracks, will it matter, provided I find a safe hiding-place inside the town?"

"And wait in the cold of the night? You would freeze before morning. No, let me think. We can do better for you than that."

Her lips shaped: *"We?"* in silence, wondering, but quick to understand. She did not question his decisions, as he had not questioned hers. He thought he would long remember the slow, deepening smile, the glow of warmth mantling her cheeks. "You believe me!" she said.

"Every word! Here, give me the candlesticks, let me wrap them, and do you put up your hair again in net and hood. We've had no fresh snow since morning, the path to the parish door is well trodden, no one will know your tracks among the many. And, girl, when you come to the town end of the bridge there's a little house off to the left, under the wall, close to the town gate. Knock there and ask for shelter over the night till the gates open, and say that Brother Cadfael sent you. They know me, I doctored their son when he was sick. They'll give you a warm corner and a place to lie, for kindness' sake, and ask no questions, and answer none from others, either. And likely they'll know where to find the silversmiths of the town, to set you on your way."

She bound up her pale, bright hair and covered her head, wrapping the cloak about her, and was again the maidservant in homespun. She obeyed without question his every word, moved silently at his back round the great court by way of the shadows, halting when he halted, and so he brought her to the church, and let her out by the parish door into the public street, still a good hour before Matins. At the last moment she said, close at his shoulder within the half-open door. "I shall be grateful always. Some day I shall send you word."

"No need for words," said Brother Cadfael, "if you send me the sign I shall be waiting for. Go now, quickly, there's not a soul stirring."

She was gone, lightly and silently, flitting past the abbey gatehouse like a tall shadow, towards the bridge and the town. Cadfael closed the door softly, and went back up the night stairs to the dortoir, too late to sleep, but in good time to rise at the sound of the bell, and return in procession to celebrate Matins.

There was, of course, the resultant uproar to face next morning, and he could not afford to avoid it, there was too much at stake. Lady FitzHamon naturally expected her maid to be in attendance as soon as she opened her eyes, and raised a petulant outcry when there was no submissive shadow waiting to dress her and do her hair. Calling failed to summon and search to find Elfgiva, but it was an hour or more before it dawned on the lady that she had lost her accomplished maid for good. Furiously she made her own toilet, unassisted, and raged out to complain to her husband, who had risen before her, and was waiting for her to accompany him to Mass. At her angry declaration that Elfgiva was nowhere to be found, and must have run away during the night, he first scoffed, for why should a sane girl take herself off into a killing frost when she had warmth and shelter and enough to eat where she was? Then he made the inevitable connection, and let out a roar of rage.

"Gone, is she? And my candlesticks gone with her, I dare swear! So it was *she*! The foul little thief! But I'll have her yet, I'll drag her back, she shall not live to enjoy her ill-gotten gains. . . ."

It seemed likely that the lady would heartily endorse all this; her mouth was already open to echo him when Brother Cadfael, brushing her sleeve close as the agitated brothers ringed the pair, contrived to shake a few grains of lavender onto her wrist. Her mouth closed abruptly. She gazed at the tiny things for the briefest instant before she shook them off, she flashed an even briefer glance at Brother Cadfael, caught his eye, and heard in a rapid whisper: "Madam, softly!—proof of the maid's innocence is also proof of the mistress's."

She was by no means a stupid woman. A second quick glance confirmed what she had already grasped, that there was one man here who had a weapon to hold over her at least as deadly as any she could use against Elfgiva. She was also a woman of decision, and wasted no time in bitterness once her course was chosen. The tone in which she addressed her lord was almost as sharp as that in which she had complained of Elfgiva's desertion.

"She your thief, indeed! That's folly, as you should very well know. The girl is an ungrateful fool to leave me, but a thief she never has been, and certainly is not this time. She can't possibly have taken the candlesticks, you know well enough when they vanished, and you know I was not well that night, and went early to bed. She was with me until long after Brother Prior discovered the theft. I asked her to stay with me until you came to bed. *As you never did!*" she ended tartly. "You may remember!"

Hamo probably remembered very little of that night; certainly he was in no position to gainsay what his wife so roundly declared. He took out a little of his ill-temper on her, but she was not so much in awe of him that she dared not reply in kind. Of course she was certain of what she said! *She* had not drunk herself stupid at the lord abbot's table, she

had been nursing a bad head of another kind, and even with Brother Cadfael's remedies she had not slept until after midnight, and Elfgiva had then been still beside her. Let him hunt a runaway maidservant, by all means, the thankless hussy, but never call her a thief, for she was none.

Hunt her he did, though with less energy now it seemed clear he would not recapture his property with her. He sent his grooms and half the lay servants off in both directions to enquire if anyone had seen a solitary girl in a hurry; they were kept at it all day, but they returned empty-handed.

The party from Lidyate, less one member, left for home next day. Lady FitzHamon rode demurely behind young Madoc, her cheek against his broad shoulders; she even gave Brother Cadfael the flicker of a conspiratorial smile as the cavalcade rode out of the gates, and detached one arm from round Madoc's waist to wave as they reached the roadway. So Hamo was not present to hear when Brother Jordan, at last released from his vow, told how Our Lady had appeared to him in a vision of light, fair as an angel, and taken away with her the candlesticks that were hers to take and do with as she would, and how she had spoken to him, and enjoined on him his three days of silence. And if there were some among the listeners who wondered whether the fair woman had not been a more corporeal being, no one had the heart to say so to Jordan, whose vision was comfort and consolation for the fading of the light.

That was at Matins, at midnight of the day of St. Stephen's. Among the scattering of alms handed in at the gatehouse next morning for the beggars, there was a little basket that weighed surprisingly heavily. The porter could not remember who had brought it, taking it to be some offerings of food or old clothing, like all the rest; but when it was opened it sent Brother Oswald, almost incoherent with joy and wonder, running to Abbot Heribert to report what seemed to be a miracle. For the basket was full of gold coin, to the value of more than a hundred marks. Well used, it would ease all the worst needs of his poorest petitioners, until the weather relented.

"Surely," said Brother Oswald devoutly, "Our Lady has made her own will known. Is not this the sign we have hoped for?"

Certainly it was for Cadfael, and earlier than he had dared to hope for it. He had the message that needed no words. She had found him, and been welcomed with joy. Since midnight Alard the silversmith had been a free man, and free man makes free wife. Presented with such a woman as Elfgiva, he could give as gladly as she, for what was gold, what was silver, by comparison?

Eye Witness

t was undoubtedly inconsiderate of Brother Ambrose to fall ill with a raging quinsy just a few days before the yearly rents were due for collection, and leave the rolls still uncopied, and the new entries still to be made. No one knew the abbey rolls as Brother Ambrose did. He had been clerk to Brother Matthew, the cellarer, for four years, during which time fresh grants to the abbey had been flooding in richly: a new mill on the Tern, pastures, assarts, messuages in the town, glebes in the countryside, a fishery up-river, even a church or two, and there was no one who could match him at putting a finger on the slippery tenant or the field-lawyer, or the householder who had always three good stories to account for his inability to pay. And here was the collection only a day away, and

Brother Ambrose on his back in the infirmary, croaking like a sick raven, and about as much use.

Brother Matthew's chief steward, who always made the collection within the town and suburbs of Shrewsbury in person, took it almost as a personal injury. He had had to install as substitute a young lay clerk who had entered the abbey service not four months previously. Not that he had found any cause to complain of the young man's work. He had copied industriously and neatly, and shown great alertness and interest in his quick grasp of what he copied, making round, respectful eyes at the value of the rent-roll.

But Master William Rede had been put out, and was bent on letting everyone know of it. He was a querulous, argumentative man in his fifties, who, if you said white to him, would inevitably say black, and bring documentary evidence to back up his contention. He came to visit his old friend and helper in the abbey infirmary, the day before the town collection was due, but whether to comfort or reproach was matter for speculation. Brother Ambrose, still voiceless, essayed speech and achieved only a painful wheeze, before Brother Cadfael, who was anointing his patient's throat afresh with goose-grease, and had a soothing syrup of orpine standing by, laid a palm over the sufferer's mouth and ordered silence.

"Now, William," he said tolerantly, "if you can't comfort, don't vex. This poor soul's got you on his conscience as it is, and you know, as well as I do, that you have the whole matter at your finger-ends. You tell him so, and fetch up a smile, or out you go." And he wrapped a length of good Welsh flannel round the glistening throat, and reached for the spoon that stood in the beaker of syrup. Brother Ambrose opened his mouth with the devoted resignation of a little bird waiting to be fed, and sucked in the dose with an expression of slightly surprised appreciation.

But William Rede was not going to be done out of his grievance so easily. "Oh, no fault of yours," he owned grudgingly, "but very ill luck for me, as if I had not enough on my hands in any event, with the rent-roll grown so long, and the burden of scribe's work for ever lengthening, as it does. And I have troubles of my own nearer home, into the bargain, with that rogue son of mine nothing but brawler and gamester as he is. If I've told him once I've told him a score of times, the next time he comes to me to pay his debts or buy him out of trouble, he'll come in vain, he may sweat it out in gaol, and serve him right. A man would think he could get a little peace and comfort from his own flesh and blood. All I get is vexation."

Once launched upon this tune, he was liable to continue the song indefinitely, and Brother Ambrose was already looking apologetic and abject, as though not William, but he, had engendered the unsatisfactory son. Cadfael could not recall that he had ever spoken with young Rede, beyond exchanging the time of day, and knew enough about fathers and sons, and the expectations each had of the other, to take all such complaints with wary reserve. Report certainly said the young man was a wild one, but at twenty-two which of the town hopefuls was not? By thirty they were most of them working hard, and minding their own purses, homes and wives.

"Your lad will mend, like many another," said Cadfael comfortably, edging the voluble visitor out from the infirmary into the sunshine of the great court. Before them on their left the great west tower of the church loomed; on their right, the long block of the guest-halls, and beyond, the crowns of the garden trees just bursting into leaf and bud, with a moist, pearly light filming over stonework and cobbles and all with a soft Spring sheen. "And as for the rents, you know very well, old humbug, that you have your finger on every line of the leiger book, and tomorrow's affair will go like a morning walk. At any rate, you can't complain of your prentice hand. He's worked hard enough over those books of yours."

"Jacob has certainly shown application," the steward agreed cautiously. "I own I've been surprised at the grasp he has of abbey affairs, in so short a time. Young people nowadays take so little interest in what they're set to do—fly-by-nights and frivolous, most of them. It's been heartening to see one of them work with such zeal. I daresay he knows the value due from every property of the house by this time. Yes, a good boy. But too ingenuous, Cadfael, there's his flaw—too affable. Figures and characters on vellum cannot baffle him, but a rogue with a friendly tongue might come over him. He cannot stand men off—he cannot put frost between. It's not well to be too open with all men."

It was mid-afternoon; in an hour or so it would be time for Vespers. The great court had always some steady flow of activity, but at this hour it was at its quietest. They crossed the court together at leisure, Brother Cadfael to return to his workshop in the herb garden, the steward to the north walk of the cloister, where his assistant was hard at work in the scriptorium. But before they had reached the spot where their paths would divide, two young men emerged from the cloister in easy conversation, and came towards them.

Jacob of Bouldon was a sturdy, square-set young fellow from the south of the shire, with a round, amiable face, large, candid eyes, and a ready smile. He came with a vellum leaf doubled in one hand, and a pen behind his ear, in every particular the eager, hard-working clerk. A little too open to any man's approaches, perhaps, as his master had said. The lanky, narrow-headed fellow attentive at his side had a very different look about him, weather-beaten, sharp-eyed and drab in hard-wearing dark clothes, with a leather jerkin to bear the rubbing of a heavy pack. The back of the left shoulder was scrubbed pallid and dull from much carrying, and his hat was wide and drooping of brim, to shed off rain. A travelling haberdasher with a few days' business in Shrewsbury, no novelty in the commoners' guest-hall of the abbey. His like were always on the roads, somewhere about the shire.

The pedlar louted to Master William with obsequious respect, said his goodday, and made off to his lodging. Early to be home for the night, surely, but perhaps he had done good business and come back to replenish his stock. A wise tradesman kept something in reserve, when he had a safe store to hand, rather than carry his all on every foray.

Master William looked after him with no great favour. "What had that fellow to do thus with you, boy?" he questioned suspiciously. "He's a deal too curious, with that long nose of his. I've seen him making up to any of the household he can back into a corner. What was he after in the scriptorium?"

Jacob opened his wide eyes even wider. "Oh, he's an honest fellow enough, sir, I'm sure. Though he does like to probe into everything, I grant you, and asks a lot of questions. . . ."

"Then you give him no answers," said the steward firmly.

"I don't, nothing but general talk that leaves him no wiser. Though I think he's but naturally inquisitive and no harm meant. He likes to curry favour with everyone, but that's by way of his trade. A rough-tongued pedlar would not sell many tapes and laces," said the young man blithely, and flourished the leaf of vellum he carried. "I was coming to ask you about this carucate of land in Recordine—there's an erasure in the leiger book, I looked up the copy to compare. You'll remember sir, it was disputed land for a while, the heir tried to recover it. . . ."

"I do recall. Come, I'll show you the original copy. But have as little to say to these travelling folk as you can with civility," Master William adjured earnestly. "There are rogues on the roads as well as honest tradesmen. There, you go before, I'll follow you."

He looked after the jaunty figure as it departed smartly, back to the scriptorium. "As I said, Cadfael, too easily pleased with every man. It's not wise to look always for the best in men. But for all that," he added, reverting morosely to his private grievance, "I wish that scamp of mine was more like him. In debt already for some gambling folly, and he has to get himself picked up by the sergeants for a street brawl, and fined, and cannot pay the fine. And to keep my own name in respect, he's confident I shall have to buy him clear. I must see to it tomorrow, one way or the other, when I've finished my rounds in the town, for he has but three days left to pay. If it weren't for his mother . . . Even so, even so, this time I ought to let him stew."

He departed after his clerk, shaking his head bitterly over his troubles. And Cadfael went off to see what feats of idiocy or genius Brother Oswin had wrought in the herb garden in his absence.

* * *

In the morning, when the brothers came out from Prime, Brother Cadfael saw the steward departing to begin his round, the deep leather satchel secured to his locked belt, and swinging by two stout straps. By evening it would be heavy with the annual wealth of the city rents, and those from the northern suburbs outside the walls. Jacob was there to see him go, listening dutifully to his last emphatic instructions, and sighing as he was left behind to complete the bookwork. Warin Harefoot, the packman, was off early, too, to ply his trade among the housewives either of the town or the parish of the Foregate. A pliable fellow, full of professional bows and smiles, but by the look of him all his efforts brought him no better than a meagre living.

So there went Jacob, back to his pen and inkhorn in the cloisters, and forth to his important business went Master William. And who knows, thought Cadfael, which is in the right, the young man who sees the best in all, and trusts all, or the old one who suspects all until he has probed them through and through? The one may stumble into a snare now and then, but at least enjoy sunshine along the way, between falls. The other may never miss his footing, but seldom experience joy. Better find a way somewhere between!

It was a curious chance that seated him next to Brother Eutropius at breakfast, for what did anyone know about Brother Eutropius? He had come to the abbey of Saint Peter and Saint Paul of Shrewsbury only two months ago, from a minor grange of the order. But in two months of Brother Oswin, say, that young man would have been an open book to every reader, whereas Eutropius contained himself as tightly as did his skin, and gave out much less in the way of information. A taciturn man, thirty or so at a guess, who

kept himself apart and looked solitary discontent at everything that crossed his path, but never complained. It might
be merely newness and shyness, in one naturally uncommu-
nicative, or it might be a gnawing inward anger against his
lot and all the world. Rumour said, a man frustrated in love,
and finding no relief in his resort to the cowl. But rumour
was using its imagination, for want of fuel more reliable.

Eutropius also worked under Brother Matthew, the cel-
larer, and was intelligent and literate, but not a good or a
quick scribe. Perhaps, when Brother Ambrose fell ill, he
would have liked to be trusted to take over his books. Perhaps he resented the lay clerk being preferred before him.
Perhaps! With Eutropius everything, thus far, was conjecture. Some day someone would pierce that carapace of his,
with an unguarded word or a sudden irresistible motion of
grace, and the mystery would no longer be a mystery, or the
stranger a stranger.

Brother Cadfael knew better than to be in a hurry, where
souls were concerned. There was plenty of elbow-room in
eternity.

In the afternoon, returning to the grange court to collect
some seed he had left stored in the loft, Cadfael encountered
Jacob, his scribing done for the moment, setting forth impor-
tantly with his own leather satchel into the Foregate.

"So he's left you a parcel to clear for him," said Cadfael.

"I would gladly have done more," said Jacob, mildly
aggrieved and on his dignity. He looked less than his
twenty-five years, well-grown as he was, with that cherubic
face. "But he says I'm sure to be slow, not knowing the
rounds or the tenants, so he's let me take only the outlying
lanes here in the Foregate, where I can take my time. I

daresay he's right, it will take me longer than I think. I'm sorry to see him so worried about his son," he said, shaking his head. "He has to see to this business with the law, he told me not to worry if he was late returning today. I hope all goes well," said the loyal subordinate, and set forth sturdily to do his own duty towards his master, however beset he might be by other cares.

Cadfael took his seed back to the garden, put in an hour or so of contented work there, washed his hands, and went to check on the progress of Brother Ambrose, who was just able to croak in his ear, more audibly than yesterday: "I could rise and help poor William—such a day for him. . . ."

He was halted there by a large, rough palm. "Lie quiet," said Cadfael, "like a wise man. Let them see how well they can fend without you, and they'll value you the better hereafter. And about time, too!" And he fed his captive bird again, and returned to his labours in the garden.

At Vespers, Brother Eutropius came late and in haste, and took his place breathing rapidly, but as impenetrable as ever. And when they emerged to go to supper in the refectory, Jacob of Bouldon was just coming in at the gatehouse with his leather satchel of rents jealously guarded by one hand and looking round hopefully for his master, who had not yet returned. Nor had he some twenty minutes later, when supper was over; but in the gathering dusk Warin Harefoot trudged wearily across the court to the guest-hall, and the pack on his shoulder looked hardly lighter than when he had gone out in the morning.

Madog of the Dead-Boat, in addition to his primary means of livelihood, which was salvaging dead bodies from the River Severn at any season, had a number of seasonal occupations that afforded him sport as well as a living. Of these the one he enjoyed most was fishing, and of all the fishing seasons the one he liked best was the early Spring run up-river of the mature salmon, fine, energetic young males which had arrived early in the estuary, and would run and leap like athletes many miles upstream before they spawned. Madog was expert at taking them, and had had one out of the water this same day, before he paddled his coracle into the thick bushes under the castle's watergate, a narrow lane running down from the town, and dropped a lesser line into the river to pick up whatever else offered. Here he was in good, leafy cover, and could stake himself into the bank and lie back to drowse until his line jerked him awake. From above, whether castle ramparts, town wall or upper window, he could not be seen.

It was beginning to grow dusk when he was startled wide awake by the hollow splash of something heavy plunging into the water, just upstream. Alert in a moment, he shoved off a yard or so from shore to look that way, but saw nothing to account for the sound, until an eddy in midstream showed him a dun-coloured sleeve breaking surface, and then the oval pallor of a face rising and sinking again from sight. A man's body turned slowly in the current as it sailed past. Madog was out after it instantly, his paddle plying. Getting a body from the river into a coracle is a tricky business, but he had practised it so long that he had it perfect, balance and heft and all, from his first grasp on the billowing sleeve to the moment when the little boat bobbed like a cork and spun like a drifting leaf, with the drowned man in-board and stream-ing water. They were halfway across the river by that time, and there were half a dozen lay brothers just leaving their work in the vegetable gardens along the Gaye, on the other

side, the nearest help in view. Madog made for their shore, and sent a halloo ahead of him to halt their departure and bring them running.

He had the salvaged man out on the bank by the time they reached him, and had turned him face-down into the grass and hoisted him firmly by the middle to shake the water out of him, squeezing energetically with big, gnarled hands.

"He's been in the river no more than a breath or two. I heard him souse into the water. Did you see ought over there by the water-gate?" But they shook their heads, concerned and anxious, and stooped to the drenched body, which at that instant heaved in breath, choked, and vomited the water it had swallowed. "He's breathing. He'll do. But he was meant to drown, sure enough. See here!"

On the back of the head of thick, greying hair blood slowly seeped, along a broken and indented wound.

One of the lay brothers exclaimed aloud, and kneeled to turn up to the light the streaked and pallid face. "Master William! This is our steward! He was collecting rents in the town. . . . See, the pouch is gone from his belt!" Two rubbed and indented spots showed where the heavy satchel had bruised the leather beneath, and the lower edge of the stout belt itself showed a nick from a sharp knife, where the thongs had been sliced through in haste. "Robbery and murder!"

"The one, surely, but not the other—not yet," said Madog practically. "He's breathing, you've not lost him yet. But we'd best get him to the nearest and best-tended bed, and that'll be in your infirmary, I take it. Make use of those hoes and spades of yours, lads, and here's a coat of mine to spare, if some of you will give up yours. . . ."

They made a litter to carry Master William back to the

abbey, as quickly and steadily as they could. Their entry at the gatehouse brought out porters, guests, and brothers in alarm and concern. Brother Edmund the infirmarer came running and led the way to a bed beside the fire in the sick quarters. Jacob of Bouldon, rushing to confirm his fears, set up a distressed cry, but recovered himself gallantly, and ran for Brother Cadfael. The sub-prior, once informed of the circumstances by Madog, who was too accustomed to drowned and near-drowned men to get excited, sensibly sent a messenger hot-foot into the town to tell provost and sheriff what had happened, and the hunt was up almost before the victim was stripped of his soaked clothes, rolled in blankets and put to bed.

The sheriff's sergeant came, and listened to Madog's tale, with only a momentary narrowing of eyes at the fleeting suspicion that the tough old Welsh waterman might be adept at putting men into the water, as well as pulling them out. But in that case he would have been more likely to make sure that his victim went under, unless he was certain he could not name or identify his attacker. Madog saw the moment of doubt, and grinned scornfully.

"I get my living better ways. But if you need to question, there must be some among those gardeners from the Gaye who saw me come down-river and drop my line in under the trees there, and can tell you I never set foot ashore until I brought this one over, and shouted them to come and help with him. Maybe you don't know me, but these brothers do."

The sergeant, surely one of the few new enough to service in Shrewsbury castle to be ignorant of Madog's special position along the river, accepted Brother Edmund's warm assurances, and shrugged off his doubts.

"But sorry I am," allowed Madog, mollified, "that I neither

saw nor heard anything until he plumped into the water, for
I was drowsing. All I can say is that he went in upstream of
me, but not far—I'd say someone slid him in from the cover
of the water-gate."

"A narrow, dark place, that," said the sergeant.

"And a warren of passages above. And the light fading,
though not far gone . . . Well, maybe when he comes
round he'll be able to tell you something—he may have seen
the man that did it."

The sergeant settled down resignedly to wait for Master
William to stir, which so far he showed no sign of doing.
Cadfael had cleaned and bandaged the wound, dressing it
with a herbal salve, and the steward lay with eyes closed and
sunken, mouth painfully open upon snoring breath. Madog
reclaimed his coat, which had been drying before the fire,
and shrugged into it placidly. "Let's hope nobody's thought
the time right to help himself to my fish while my back was
turned." He had wrapped his salmon in an armful of wet
grass and covered it with his upturned boat. "I'll bid you
goodnight, brothers, and wish your sick man hale again—
and his pouch recovered, too, though that I doubt."

From the infirmary doorway he turned back to say: "You
have a patient lad here sitting shivering on the doorstep,
waiting for word. Can he not come in and see his master, he
says. I've told him the man's likely to live his old age out
with no worse than a dunt on the head to show for it, and
he'd best be off to his bed, for he'll get nothing here as yet.
Would you want him in?"

Cadfael went out with him to shoo away any such pre-
mature visits. Jacob of Bouldon, pale and anxious, was sitting with arms folded closely round his drawn-up knees,
hunched against the chill of the night. He looked up hope-

fully as they came out to him, and opened his mouth eagerly to plead. Madog clouted him amiably on the shoulder as he passed, and made off towards the gatehouse, a squat, square figure, brown and crusty as the bole of an oak.

"You'd best be off, too, into the warm," said Brother Cadfael, not unkindly. "Master William will recover well enough, but he's likely to be without his wits some time yet, no call for you to catch your death here on the stone."

"I couldn't rest," said Jacob earnestly. "I told him, I begged him, take me with you, you should have someone. But he said, folly, he had collected rents for the abbey many years, and never felt any need for a guard. And now, see. . . . Could I not come in and sit by him? I'd make no sound, never trouble him. . . . He has not spoken?"

"Nor will for some hours yet, and even then I doubt he can tell us much. I'm here with him in case of need, and Brother Edmund is on call. The fewer about him, the better."

"I'll wait a little while yet," said Jacob, fretting, and hugged his knees the tighter.

Well, if he would, he would, but cramp and cold would teach him better sense and more patience. Cadfael went back to his vigil, and closed the door. Still, it was no bad thing to encounter one lad whose devotion gave the lie to Master William's forebodings concerning the younger generation.

Before midnight there was another visitor enquiring. The porter opened the door softly and came in to whisper that Master William's son was here, asking after his father and wanting to come in and see him. Since the sergeant, departing when it seemed certain his vigil was fruitless until morning, had pledged himself to go and reassure Mistress Rede that her man was alive, well cared for, and certain to make a good recovery, Cadfael might well have gone out to bid the young man go home and take care of his mother rather than waste his time here, if the young man had not forestalled him by making a silent and determined entry on his herald's heels. A tall, shock-headed, dark-eyed youth, hunched of shoulder just now, and grim of face, but admittedly very quiet in movement, and low-voiced. His look was by no means tender or solicitous. His eyes went at once to the figure in the bed, sweaty-browed now, and breathing somewhat more easily and naturally. He brooded, glaring, and wasting no time on question or explanation, said in a level whisper: "I will stay." And with aggressive composure stayed, settling himself on the bench beside his father's bed, his two long, muscular hands gripped tightly between his knees.

The porter met Cadfael's eye, hoisted his shoulders, and went quietly away. Cadfael sat down on the other side of the bed, and contemplated the pair, father and son. Both faces looked equally aloof and critical, even hostile, yet there they were, close and quiet together.

The young man asked but two questions, each after a long silence. The first, uttered almost grudgingly, was: "Will it be well with him?" Cadfael, watching the easing flow of breath and the faint flush of colour, said simply: "Yes. Only give him time." The second was: "He has not spoken yet?"

"Not yet," said Cadfael.

Now which of those, he wondered, was the more vital question? There was one man, somewhere, who must at this moment be very anxious indeed about what William Rede might have to say, when he did speak.

The young man—his name was Edward, Cadfael recalled, after the Confessor—Eddi Rede sat all night long almost motionless, brooding over his father's bed. Most of the time, and certainly every time he had been aware of being watched in his turn, he had been scowling.

Well before Prime the sergeant was back again to his watch, and Jacob was again hovering unhappily about the doorway, peering in anxiously whenever it was opened, but not quite venturing to come in until he was invited. The sergeant eyed Eddi very hard and steadily, but said no word to disturb the injured man's increasingly restful sleep. It was past seven when at last Master William stirred, opened vague eyes, made a few small sounds which were not yet words, and tried feebly to put up a hand to his painful head, startled by the sudden twinge when he moved. The sergeant stooped close, but Cadfael laid a restraining hand on his arm.

"Give him time! A knock on the head like that will have addled his wits. We'll need to tell him things before he tells us any." And to the wondering patient he said tranquilly: "You know me—Cadfael. Edmund will be here to relieve me as soon as Prime is over. You're in his care, in the infirmary, and past the worst. Fret for nothing, lie still and let others do that. You've had a mighty dunt on the crown, and a dowsing in the river, but both are past, and thanks be, you're safe enough now."

The wandering hand reached its goal this time. Master William groaned and stared indignant surprise, and his eyes cleared and sharpened, though his voice was weak as he complained, with quickening memory: "He came behind me—someone—out of an open yard door. . . . That's the last I know. . . ." Sudden realisation shook him; he gave a stricken howl, and tried to rise from his pillow, but gave up at the pang it cost him. "The rents—the abbey rents!"

"Your life's better worth than the abbey rents," said Cadfael heartily, "and even they may be regained."

"The man who felled you," said the sergeant, leaning close, "cut your satchel loose with a knife, and made off with it. But if you can help us we'll lay him by the heels yet. Where was this that he struck you down?"

"Not a hundred paces from my own house," lamented William bitterly. "I went there when I had finished, to check my rolls and make all fast, and . . ." He shut his mouth grimly on the overriding reason. Hazily he had been aware all this time of the silent and sullen young man sitting beside him, now he fixed his eyes on him until his vision cleared. The mutual glare was spirited, and came of long practice. "What are you doing here?" he demanded.

"Waiting to have better news of you to take to my mother," said Eddi shortly. He looked up defiantly into the sergeant's face. "He came home to read me all my sins over, and warn me that the fine that's due from me in two days more is my burden now, not his, and if I can't make shift for it on my own I may go to gaol, and pay in another coin. Or it may be," he added with grudging fairness, "that he came rather to flay me and then pay my dues, as he's done more than once. But I was in no mind to listen, and he was in no mind to be flouted, so I flung out and went down to the butts. And won the good half of what I owe, for what that's worth."

"So this was a bitter quarrel you had between you," said the sergeant, narrowing suspicious eyes. "And not long after it you, master, went out to bring your rents home, and were set upon, robbed, and left for dead. And now you, boy, have the half of what you need to stay out of prison."

Cadfael, watching father and son, felt that it had not even occurred to Eddi, until then, that he might fall under suspicion of this all too opportune attack; and further, that even now it had not dawned on Master William that such a thought could occur to any sane man. He was scowling at his son for no worse reason than old custom and an aching head.

"Why are you not looking after your mother at home?" he demanded querulously.

"So I will, now I've seen and heard you more like yourself. Mother's well enough cared for, Cousin Alice is with her. But she'll be the better for knowing that you're still the same cantankerous worrit, and likely to be a plague to us twenty years yet. I'll go," said Eddi grimly, "when I'm let. But he wants your witness before he can leave you to your rest. Better get it said."

Master William submitted wearily, knitting his brows in the effort to remember. "I came from the house, along the passage towards Saint Mary's, above the water-gate. The door of the tanner's yard was standing open, I know—I'd passed it. . . . But I never heard a step behind me. As if the wall had fallen on me! I recall nothing after, except sudden cold, deadly cold. . . . Who brought me back, then, that I'm snug here?"

They told him, and he shook his head helplessly over the great blank between.

"You think the fellow must have been hiding behind that yard-door, lying in wait?"

"So it seems."

"And you caught never a glimpse? Never had time to turn your head? You can tell us nothing to trace him? Not even a guess at his build? His age?"

Nothing. Simply, there had been early dusk before him, his own steps the only sound, no man in sight between the high walls of gardens, yards and warehouses going down to the river, and then the shock of the blow, and abrupt darkness. He was growing tired again, but his mind was clear enough. There would be no more to get from him.

Brother Edmund came in, eyed his patient, and silently nodded the visitors out at the door, to leave him in peace. Eddi kissed his father's dangling hand, but brusquely, rather as though he would as lief have bitten it, and marched out to blink at the sunlight in the great court. With a face grimly defiant he waited for the sergeant's dismissal.

"I left him as I told you, I went to the butts, and played into a wager there, and shot well. You'll want names from me. I can give them. And I'm still short the half of my fine, for what that's worth. I knew nothing of this until I went home, and that was late, after your messenger had been there. Can I go home? I'm at your disposal."

"You can," granted the sergeant, so readily that it was clear the young man would not be unwatched on the way, or on arrival. "And there stay, for I shall want more from you than merely names. I'm away to take their tales from the lay brothers who were working late at the Gaye yesterday, but I'll not be long after you in the town."

The workers were already assembling in the court and moving off to their day's labour. The sergeant strode forth to find his men, and left Eddi glowering after him, and Cadfael mildly observing the wary play of thought in the dark young face. Not a bad-looking lad, if he would wear a sunnier visage; but perhaps at this moment he had little cause.

"He will truly be a hale man again?" he asked suddenly, turning his black gaze on Cadfael.

"As whole and hearty as ever he was."

"And you'll take good care of him?"

"So we will," agreed Cadfael innocently, "even though he may be a cantankerous worrit and a plague."

"I'm sure none of you here have any call to say so," flashed the young man with abrupt ferocity. "The abbey has had loyal and solid service from him all these years, and owes him more thanks than abuse." And he turned his back and stalked away out of the great court, leaving Cadfael looking after him with a thoughtful face and the mere trace of a smile.

He was careful to wipe off the smile before he went back to Master William, who was in no mood to take himself, his son and his troubles anything but seriously. He lay trying to blink and frown away his headache, and fulminating about his offspring in a glum undertone.

"You see what I have to complain of, who should be able to look for comfort and support at home. A wild, unbiddable good-for-nothing, and insolent into the bargain . . ."

"So he is," agreed Cadfael sympathetically, wooden-faced. "No wonder you mean to let him pay for his follies in prison, and small blame to you."

He got an acid glare as reward. "I shall do no such thing!" snapped Master William sharply. "The boy's no worse than you or I at his age, I daresay. Nothing wrong with him that time won't cure."

Master William's disaster, it seemed, had shaken the serenity of the abbey from choir to guest-hall. The enquiries were many and assiduous. Young Jacob had been hopping about outside the infirmary from dawn, unable to tear himself away even to the duties he owed his injured master, until Cadfael had taken pity on his obvious anxiety, and stopped to tell him that there was no need for such distress, for the worst was over, and all would be well with Master William.

"You are sure, brother? He has regained his senses? He has spoken? His mind is clear?"

Patiently Cadfael repeated his reassurances.

"But such villainy! Has he been able to help the sheriff's men? Did he see his attacker? Has he any notion who it could have been?"

"Not that, no. Never a glimpse, he was struck from behind, and knew no more until he came to this morning in the infirmary. He's no help to the law, I fear. It was not to be expected."

"But he himself will be well and strong again?"

"As ever he was, and before long, too."

"Thank God, brother!" said Jacob fervently, and went away satisfied to his accounts. For even with the town rents lost, there was still bookwork to be done on what remained.

More surprising it seemed to be stopped on the way to the dortoir by Warin Harefoot, the haberdasher, with a very civil enquiry after the steward's health. Warin did not presume to display the agitation of a favoured colleague like Jacob, but rather the mannerly sympathy of a humble guest of the house, and the law-abiding citizen's indignation at evil-doing, and desire that justice should pursue the evildoer. Had his honour been able to put a name or a face to his attacker? A great pity! Yet justice, he hoped, might still be done. And would there—should any man be so fortunate as to trace the missing satchel with its treasure—would there be a small reward for such a service? To an honest man who restored it, Cadfael thought, there well might. Warin went off to his day's peddling in Shrewsbury, humping his heavy pack. The back view of him, for some reason, looked both purposeful and jaunty.

But the strangest and most disturbing enquirer made, in fact, no enquiry, but came silently in, as Cadfael was paying another brief visit to the infirmary in the early afternoon, after catching up with some of his lost sleep. Brother Eutropius stood motionless and intent at the foot of the steward's bed, staring down with great hollow eyes in a face like a stone mask. He gave never a glance to Cadfael. All he regarded was the sleeping man, now so placid and eased for all his bandaged head, a man from the river, back from the grave. He stood there for a long time, his lips moving on inaudible formulae of prayer. Suddenly he shuddered, like someone waking from a trance, and crossed himself, and went away as silently as he had come.

Cadfael was so concerned at his manner and his closed face that he went out after him, no less quietly, and followed him at a distance through the cloisters and into the church.

Brother Eutropius was on his knees before the high altar, his marble face upraised over clasped hands. His eyelids were closed, but the dark lashes glittered. A handsome, agonised man of thirty, with a strong body and a fierce, tormented heart, his lips framing silently but readably in the altar-light, *"Mea culpa . . . maxima mea culpa . . ."*

Cadfael would have liked to pierce the distance and the ice between, but it was not the time. He went quietly, and left Brother Eutropius to the remnant of his disrupted solitude, for whatever had happened to him, the shell was cracked and disintegrating, and never again would he be able to reassemble it about him.

Cadfael went into the town before Vespers, to call upon Mistress Rede, and take her the latest good word of her man. It was by chance that he met the sergeant at the High Cross, and stopped to exchange news. It had been a routine precaution to round up a few of the best-known rogues in

Shrewsbury, and make them account for their movements the previous day, but that had yielded nothing. Eddi's fellow-marksmen at the butts under the town wall had sworn to his story willingly, but seeing they were all his cronies from boyhood, that meant little enough. The one new thing, and it marked the exact spot of the attack past question, was the discovery in the passage above the water-gate of the one loop of leather from Master William's pouch, the one which had been sliced clean through and left lying in the thief's haste, and the dim light under the high walls.

"Right under the clothier's cart-yard. The walls are ten feet high, and the passage narrow. Never a place from which the lane can be overlooked. No chance in the world of an eye witness. He chose his place well."

"Ah, but there *is* one place, then, from which a man might have watched the deed," said Cadfael, enlightened. "The loft above that cart-house and barn has a hatch higher than the wall, and close to it. And Roger Clothier lets Rhodri Fychan sleep up there—the old Welshman who begs at Saint Mary's church. By that time of the evening he may have been up in the hay already, and on a fine evening he'd be sitting by the open hatch. And even if he had not come home at that time, who's to be sure of that? It's enough that he *could* have been there. . . ."

He had been right about the sergeant; the man was an incomer, not yet acquainted with the half of what went on in Shrewsbury. He had not known Madog of the Dead-Boat, he did not know Rhodri Fychan. Pure chance had cast this particular affair into the hands of such a man, and perhaps no ill chance, either.

"You have given me a notion," said Cadfael, "that may bring us nearer the truth yet. Not that I'd let the old man run any risk, but no need for that. Listen, there's a baited trap we might try, if you're agreeable. If it succeeds, you may have your man. If it fails, we shall have lost nothing. But it's a matter of doing it quietly—no public proclamation, leave the baiting to me. Will you give it a trial? It's your credit if we hook our fish, and it costs but a night-watch."

The sergeant stared, already sniffing at the hope of praise and promotion, but cautious still. "What is it you have in mind?"

"Say you had done this thing, there between blind walls, and then suddenly heard that an old man slept above every night of the year, and may have been there when you struck. And say you were told that this old beggar has not yet been questioned—but tomorrow he will be. . . ."

"Brother," said the sergeant, "I am with you. I am listening."

There were two things to be done, after that, if the springe was to succeed, and imperil no one but the guilty. No need to worry, as yet, about getting permission to be absent in the night, or, failing that, making his own practised but deprecated way out without permission. Though he had confidence in Abbot Radulfus, who had, before now, shown confidence in him. Justice is a permitted passion, the just respect it. Meantime, Cadfael went up to Saint Mary's churchyard, and sought out the venerable beggar who sat beside the west door, in his privileged and honoured place.

Rhodri the Less—for his father had been Rhodri, too, and a respected beggar like his son—knew the footsteps, and turned up a wrinkled and pock-marked face, brown as the soil, smiling.

"Brother Cadfael, well met, and what's the news with you?"

Cadfael sat down beside him, and took his time. "You'll have heard of this bad business that was done right under your bedchamber, yesterday evening. Were you there, last night?"

"Not when this befell," said the old man, scratching his white poll thoughtfully, "and can find no one who was down there at that time, either. Last night I begged late, it was a mild evening. Vespers was over and gone here before I went home."

"No matter," said Cadfael. "Now listen, friend, for I'm borrowing your nest tonight, and you'll be a guest else-where, if you'll be my helper. . . ."

"For a Welshman," said the old man comfortably, "what-ever he asks. You need only tell me." But when it was told, he shook his head firmly. "There's an inner loft. In the worst of the winter I move in there for the warmth, away from the frosty air. Why should I not be present? There's a door between, and room for you and more. And I should like, Brother Cadfael, I should like of all things to be witness when Will Rede's murderer gets his come-uppance."

He leaned to rattle his begging-bowl at a pious lady who had been putting up prayers in the church. Business was business, and the pitch he held was the envy of the beggars of Shrewsbury. He blessed the giver, and reached a delaying hand to halt Cadfael, who was rising to depart.

"Brother, a word for you that might come helpfully, who knows! They are saying that one of your monks was down under the bridge yesterday evening, about the time Madog took up Will out of the water. They say he stood there under the stone a long time, like a man in a dream, but no good dream. One they know but very little, a man in his prime, dark-avised, solitary . . ."

"He came late to Vespers," said Cadfael, remembering.

"You know I have those who tell me things, for no evil purpose—a man who sits still must have the world come to him. They tell me this brother walked into the water, above his sandals, and would have gone deeper, but it was then Madog of the Dead-Boat hallooed that he had a drowned man aboard. And the strange monk drew back out of the water and fled from his devil. So they say. Does it mean anything to you?"

"Yes," said Cadfael slowly. "Yes, it means much."

When Cadfael had finished reassuring the steward's brisk, birdlike little wife that she should have her man back in a day or two as good as new, he drew Eddi out with him into the yard, and told him all that was in the wind.

"And I am off back now to drop the quiet word into a few ears I can think of, where it may raise the fiercest itch. But not too early, or why should not the thought be passed on to the sheriff's man at once for action? No, last thing, after dark, when all good brothers are making their peace with the day before bed, I shall have recalled that there's one place from which yonder lane can be overlooked, and one man who sleeps the nights there, year round, and may have things to tell. First thing tomorrow, I shall let them know, I'll send the sheriff the word, and let him deal. Whoever fears an eye witness shall have but this one night to act."

The young man eyed him with a doubtful face but a glint in his glance. "Since you can hardly expect to take *me* in that trap, brother, I reckon you have another use for me."

"This is your father. If you will, you may be with the witnesses in the rear loft. But mark, I do not know, no one can know yet, that the bait will fetch any man."

"And if it does not," said Eddi with a wry grin, "if no one comes, I can still find the hunt hard on my heels."

"True! But if it succeeds . . ."

He nodded grimly. "Either way, I have nothing to lose. But listen, one thing I want amended, or I'll spring your trap before the time. It is not I who will be in the rear loft with Rhodri Fychan and your sergeant. It is *you*. I shall be the sleeper in the straw, waiting for a murderer. You said rightly, brother—this is *my* father. Mine, not yours!"

This had been no part of Brother Cadfael's plans, but for all that, he found it did not greatly surprise him. Nor, by the set of the intent young face and the tone of the quiet voice, did he think demur would do much good. But he tried.

"Son, since it *is* your father, think better of it. He'll have need of you. A man who has tried once to kill will want to make certain this time. He'll come with a knife, if he comes at all. And you, however sharp your ears and stout your heart, still at a disadvantage, lying in a feigned sleep. . . ."

"And are your senses any quicker than mine, and your sinews any suppler and stronger?" Eddi grinned suddenly, and clapped him on the shoulder with a large and able hand. "Never fret, brother, I am well prepared for when that man and I come to grips. You go and sow your good seed, and may it bear fruit! I'll make ready."

When robbery and attempted murder are but a day and a half old, and still the sensation of a whole community, it is by no means difficult to introduce the subject and insert into the speculations whatever new crumb of interest you may wish to propagate. As Cadfael found, going about his private business in the half-hour after Compline. He did not have to introduce the subject, in fact, for no one was talking about anything else. The only slight difficulty was in confiding his sudden idea to each man in solitude, since any general announcement would at once have caused some native to blurt out the obvious objection, and give the entire game away. But even that gave little trouble, for certainly the right man, if he really was among those approached, would not say one word of it to anyone else, and would have far too much to think about to want company or conversation the rest of the night.

Young Jacob, emerging cramped and yawning after hours of assiduous scribing, broken only by snatched meals and a dutiful visit to his master, now sitting up by the infirmary hearth, received Brother Cadfael's sudden idea wide-eyed and eager, and offered, indeed, to hurry to the castle even at this late hour to tell the watch about it, but Cadfael considered that hard-working officers of the law might be none too grateful at having their night's rest disrupted; and in any case nothing would be changed by morning.

To half a dozen guests of the commoners' hall, who came to make kind enquiry after Master William, he let fall his idea openly, as a simple possibility, since none of them was a Shrewsbury man, or likely to know too much about the inhabitants. Warin Harefoot was among the six, and perhaps the instigator of the civil gesture. He looked, as always, humble, zealous, and pleased at any motion, even the slightest, towards justice.

There remained one mysterious and troubled figure. Surely not a murderer, not even quite a self-murderer, though by all the signs he had come very close. But for Madog's cry of "Drowned man!" he might indeed have waded into the full flow of the stream and let it take him. It was as if God himself had set before him, like a lightning stroke from heaven, the enormity of the act he contemplated, and driven him back from the brink with the dazzle of hell-fire. But those who returned stricken and penitent to face this world had need also of men, and the communicated warmth of men.

Before Cadfael so much as opened the infirmary door, on a last visit to the patient within, he had a premonition of what he would find. Master William and Brother Eutropius sat companionably one on either side of the hearth, talking together in low, considerate voices, with silences as acceptable as speech, and speech no more eloquent than the silences. There was no defining the thread that linked them, but there would never be any breaking it. Cadfael would have withdrawn unnoticed, but the slight creak of the door drew Brother Eutropius' attention, and he rose to take his leave.

"Yes, brother, I know—I've overstayed. I'll come."

It was time to withdraw to the dortoir and their cells, and sleep the sleep of men at peace. And Eutropius, as he fell in beside Cadfael in the great court, had the face of a man utterly at peace. Drained, still dazed by the thunderbolt of revelation, but already, surely, confessed and absolved. Empty now, and still a little at a loss in reaching out a hand to a fellow-man.

"Brother, I think it was you who came into the church, this afternoon. I am sorry if I caused you anxiety. I had but newly looked my fault in the face. It seemed to me that my sin had all but killed another, an innocent, man. Brother, I have long known in my head that despair is mortal sin. Now I know it with my blood and bowels and heart."

Cadfael said, stepping delicately: "No sin is mortal, if it is deeply and truly repented. He lives, and you live. You need not see your case as extreme, brother. Many a man has fled

from grief into the cloister, only to find that grief can follow
him there."

"There was a woman. . . ." said Eutropius, his voice low,
laboured but calm. "Until now I could not speak of this. A
woman who played me false, bitterly, yet I could not leave
loving. Without her my life seemed of no worth. I know its
value better now. For the years left to me I will pay its price
in full, and carry it without complaint."

To him Cadfael said nothing more. If there was one man in
all this web of guilt and innocence who would sleep deeply
and well in his own bed that night, it was Brother Eutropius.

As for Cadfael himself, he had best make haste to take
advantage of his leave of absence, and get to the clothier's
loft by the shortest way, for it was fully dark, and if the bait
had been taken the end could not long be delayed.

The steep ladder had been left where it always leaned,
against the wall below Rhodri's hatch. In the outer loft the
darkness was not quite complete, for the square of the hatch
stood open as always on a space of starlit sky. The air within
was fresh, but warm and fragrant with the dry, heaped hay
and straw, stored from the previous summer, and dwindling
now from the winter's depredations, but still ample for a
comfortable bed. Eddi lay stretched out on his left side,
turned towards the square of luminous sky, his right arm
flung up round his head, to give him cover as he kept watch.

In the inner loft, with the door ajar between to let sounds
pass, Brother Cadfael, the sergeant, and Rhodri Fychan sat
waiting, with lantern, flint and steel ready to hand. They had
more than an hour to wait. If he was coming at all, he had
had the cold patience and self-control to wait for the thick of
the night, when sleep is deepest.

But come he did, when Cadfael, for one, had begun to
think their fish had refused the bait. It must have been
two o'clock in the morning, or past, when Eddi, watching
steadily beneath his sheltering arm, saw the level base of the
square of sky broken, as the crown of a head rose into view,
black against darkest blue, but clear to eyes already inured to
darkness. He lay braced and still, and turned his breathing to
the long, impervious rhythm of sleep, as the head rose
stealthily, and the intruder paused for a long time, head and
shoulders in view, motionless, listening. The silhouette of a
man has neither age nor colouring, only a shape. He might
have been twenty or fifty, there was no knowing. He could
move with formidable silence.

But he was satisfied. He had caught the steady sound of
breathing, and now with surprising speed mounted the last
rungs of the ladder and was in through the hatch, and the
bulk of him cut off the light. Then he was still again, to make
sure the movement had not disturbed the sleeper. Eddi was
listening no less acutely, and heard the infinitely small
whisper of steel sliding from its sheath. A dagger is the most
silent of weapons to use, but has its own voices. Eddi turned
very slightly, with wincing care, to free his left arm under
him, ready for the grapple.

The bulk and shadow, a moving darkness, mere sensation
rather than anything seen, drew close. He felt the leaning
warmth from the man's body, and the stirring of the air from
his garments, and was aware of a left hand and arm out-
stretched with care to find how he lay, hovering rather than
touching. He had time to sense how the assassin stooped,
and judge where his right hand lay waiting with the knife,
while the left selected the place to strike. Under the sacking

that covered him—for beggars do not lie in good woollens—
Eddi braced himself to meet the shock.

When the blow came, there was even a splinter of light
tracing the lunge of the blade, as the murderer drew back to
put his weight into the stroke, and uncovered half the
blessed frame of sky. Eddi flung over on his back, and took
the lunging dagger-hand cleanly by the wrist in his left hand.
He surged out of the straw ferociously, forcing the knife
away at arm's length, and with his right hand reached for
and found his opponent's throat. They rolled out of the nest
of rustling straw and across the floor, struggling, and fetched
up against the timbers of the wall. The attacker had uttered
one startled, muted cry before he was half-choked. Eddi had
made no sound at all but the fury of his movements. He let
himself be clawed by his enemy's flailing left hand, while he
laid both hands to get possession of the dagger. With all his
strength he dashed the elbow of the arm he held against the
floor. A strangled yelp answered him, the nerveless fingers
parted, and gave up the knife. Eddi sat back astride a body
suddenly limp and gasping, and laid the blade above the face
still nameless.

In the inner loft the sergeant had started up and laid hand
to the door, but Cadfael took him by the arm and held him
still.

The feverish whisper reached them clearly, but whispers
have neither sex nor age nor character. "Don't strike—wait,
listen!" He was terrified, but still thinking, still scheming. "It
is you—I know you, I've heard about you . . . his son!
Don't kill me—why should you? It wasn't you I expected—I
never meant *you* harm. . . ."

What you may have heard about him, thought Cadfael,

braced behind the door with his hand on the tinder-box he might need at any moment, may be as misleading as common report so often is. There are overtones and undertones to be listened for, that not every ear can catch.

"Lie still," said Eddi's voice, perilously calm and reasonable, "and say what you have to say where you lie. I can listen just as well with this toy at your throat. Have I said I mean to kill you?"

"But do not!" begged the eager voice, breathless and low. Cadfael knew it, now. The sergeant probably did not. In all likelihood Rhodri Fychan, leaning close and recording all, had never heard it, or he would have known it, for his ears could pick up even the shrillest note of the bat. "I can do you good. You have a fine unpaid, and only a day to run before gaol. *He* told me so. What do you owe him? He would not clear you, would he? But I can see you cleared. Listen, never say word of this, loose me and keep your own counsel, and the half is yours—the half of the abbey rents. I promise it!"

There was a blank silence. If Eddi was tempted, it was certainly not to bargain, more likely to strike, but he held his hand, at whatever cost.

"Join me," urged the voice, taking heart from his silence, "and no one need ever know. No one! They said there was a beggar slept here, but he's away, however it comes, and no one here but you and I, to know what befell. Even if they were using you, think better of it, and who's to know? Only let me go hence, and you keep a close mouth, and all's yet well, for you as well as me."

After another bleak silence Eddi's voice said with cold suspicion, "Let you loose, and you the only one who knows where you've hidden the plunder? Do you take me for a fool? I should never see my share! Tell me the place, exact, and bring me to it with you, or I give you to the law."

The listeners within felt, rather than heard, the faint sounds of writhing and struggling and baulking, like a horse resisting a rider, and then the sudden collapse, the abject surrender. "I put the money into my pouch with my own few marks," owned the voice bitterly, "and threw his satchel into the river. The money is in my bed in the abbey. No one paid any heed to my entry with the Foregate dues remaining, why should they? And those I've accounted for properly. Come down with me, and I'll satisfy you, I'll pay you. More than the half, if you'll only keep your mouth shut, and let me go free. . . ."

"You within there," suddenly bellowed Eddi, shaking with detestation, "come forth, for the love of God, and take this carrion away from under me, before I cut his villain throat, and rob the hangman of his own. Come out, and see what we've caught!"

And out they came, the sergeant to thrust across at once to bar any escape by the hatch, Cadfael to set his lantern safely on a beam well clear of the hay and straw, and tap away diligently with flint and steel until the tinder caught and glowed, and the wick burned up into a tiny flame. Eddi's captive had uttered one despairing oath, and made one frantic effort to throw off the weight that held him down and break for the open air, but was flattened back to the boards with a thump, a large, vengeful hand splayed on his chest.

"He dares, he dares," Eddi was grating through his teeth, "to try and buy my father's head from me with money—stolen money, abbey money! You heard? You heard?"

The sergeant leaned from the hatch and whistled for the two men he had had in hiding below in the barn. He was glad he had given the plan a hearing. The injured man live and mending well, the money located and safe—everything would redound to his credit. Now send the prisoner bound and helpless with his escort to the castle, and off to the abbey to unearth the money.

The guarded flame of the lantern burned up and cast a yellow light about the loft. Eddi rose and stood back from his enemy, who sat up slowly and sullenly, still breathless and bruised, and blinked round them all with the large, ingenuous eyes and round, youthful face of Jacob of Bouldon, that paragon of clerks, so quick to learn the value of a rent-roll, so earnest to win the trust and approval of his master, and lift from him every burden, particularly the burden of a full satchel of the abbey's dues.

He was grazed and dusty now, and the cheerful, lively mask had shrivelled into hostile and malevolent despair. With flickering, sidelong glances he viewed them all, and saw no way out of the circle. Longest he looked at the little, spry, bowed old man who came forth smiling at Cadfael's shoulder. For in the wrinkled, lively face the lantern-light showed two eyes that caught reflected light though they had none of their own, eyes opaque as grey pebbles and as insensitive. Jacob stared and moaned, and softly and viciously began to curse.

"Yes," said Brother Cadfael, "you might have saved yourself so vain an effort. I fear I was forced to practise a measure of deceit, which would hardly have taken in a true-born Shrewsbury man. Rhodri Fychan has been blind from birth."

It was in some way an apt ending, when Brother Cadfael and the sergeant arrived back at the abbey gatehouse, about first light, to find Warin Harefoot waiting in the porter's room for the bell for Prime to rouse the household and deliver him of his charge, which he had brought here for safety in the night. He was seated on a bench by the empty hearth, one hand clutching firmly at the neck of a coarse canvas sack.

"He has not let go of it all night," said the porter, "nor let me leave sitting t'other side of it as guard."

Warin was willing enough, however, even relieved, to hand over his responsibility to the law, with a monk of the house for witness, seeing abbot and prior were not yet up to take precedence. He undid the neck of the sack proudly, and displayed the coins within.

"You did say, brother, there might be a reward, if a man was so lucky as to find it. I had my doubts of that young clerk—I never trust a too-honest face! And if it *was* he—well, I reasoned he must hide what he stole quickly. And he had a pouch on him the like of the other, near enough, and nobody was going to wonder at seeing him wearing it, or having money in it, either, seeing he had a small round of his own. And if he came a thought late, well, he'd made a point he might make a slower job of it than he'd expected, being a novice at the collecting. So I kept my eye on him, and got my chance this night, when I saw him creep forth after dark. In his bed it was, sewn into a corner of the straw pallet. And here it is, and speak for me with the lord abbot. Trade's none so good, and a poor pedlar must live. . . ."

Gaping down at him long and wonderingly, the sergeant questioned at last: "And did you never for a moment consider slipping the whole into your own pack, and out through the gates with it in the morning?"

Warin cast up a shy, disarming glance. "Well, sir, for a moment it may be I did. But I was never the lucky sort if I did the like, never a once but I was found out. Wisdom and

experience turned me honest. Better, I hold, a small profit come by honestly than great gains gone down the wind, and me in prison for it just the same. So here's the abbey's gold again, every penny, and now I look to the lord abbot to treat a poor, decent man fair."

In 1120 A.D.
Cadfael was 40